RULES OF A RUSE

LAURA BEERS

Chapter One

England, 1814

Mr. Alden Dandridge was tired of being poor. That was the only reason why he was sitting outside his Great-aunt Edith's solicitor's office, hoping for good news. He had been waiting for what felt like hours, with only the incessant ticking of the long clock in the corner marking his misery.

Tick-tock.

When he had received word that Mr. Davidson wished to meet with him, Alden couldn't help but wonder what Great-aunt Edith was about. She was kind but eccentric, a woman he had learned to avoid over the years. So why was he here? He was hardly close to her.

Tick-tock.

Alden ran a hand through his hair. He had more important things to do with his time. Although, even he couldn't fathom his own lie. As the second son of an earl, he had no prospects, no title, and no land. His older brother, Alexander, was their father's heir and he was living the life of leisure.

How was that fair that he had been born second? A spare,

as his brother constantly reminded him. He wanted to make something of himself, but he didn't even know where to begin. His studies in Latin at Oxford seemed useless now.

Tick-tock.

That blasted clock. Why did it have to constantly remind him that he was sitting here, twiddling his thumbs, while the world continued to go on turning? It was a world of happiness that he had never known.

His eyes roamed over the small area and he saw three of his cousins waiting for the solicitor. He met Colin's eyes and tipped his head.

Colin leaned forward and asked, "Do you know what this is about?"

Alden shook his head. "I do not. I was hoping you did."

Turning his head, Colin asked their other cousins, Rose and Richard, the same question. They both shrugged, equally clueless.

Botheration.

The door to the office opened, and a short man with a thin face stuck his head out, pushing back the rounded spectacles on his face as he announced, "I apologize for the wait. Do come in."

"It is about time," Alden muttered under his breath.

He followed his cousins into the small office and saw there weren't enough chairs for him to sit so he opted to stand by the one lone window. The short man went around his desk, which was extremely meticulously tidy, with stacks of papers neatly arranged. He offered them a brief smile. "Allow me to introduce myself," he started, "my name is Mr. Davidson. I am Lady Edith Walker's solicitor."

Colin spoke up. "Why are we here?" he demanded.

Alden bobbed his head in approval. He wanted the solicitor to get straight to the point so he could get on with his day.

Mr. Davidson didn't seem perturbed by Colin's direct question. If anything, he seemed to welcome it. "I'm afraid that I am the bearer of some bad news. Lady Edith is dying."

Rose gasped. "Oh, dear," she muttered. "How much longer does Great-aunt Edith have?"

"It is hard to say," Mr. Davidson replied.

Alden stared back at the solicitor as emotions whirled inside of him. He may not have been particularly close to his great-aunt, but he didn't wish her any ill-will.

Mr. Davidson continued. "I requested this visit because Lady Edith wrote each one of you a letter." He picked up four letters from his desk. "She would like you to read them here, and I am available to answer any questions you may have."

Rising, Mr. Davidson distributed the letters and returned to his seat.

Alden looked at the small, folded letter in his hand and wondered what Great-aunt Edith could have possibly wanted to say to him. He sighed. He might as well get this over with.

He unfolded the letter and read:

My Dearest Alden,

As you have heard by now, I am dying. But that is not why I am writing this letter. It is to inform you that I want you to marry for love. For without love, life is pointless. That is why I am giving you the opportunity to do so.

I have a horse farm in Kirkcudbright, Scotland that I intend to will to you, assuming you are married by the Twelfth Night. Furthermore, and most importantly, to inherit, you must marry a young woman from the village, particularly one that is fond of horses.

The manor at the horse farm is currently occupied by a young woman that is rather dear to me- Miss Elinor Sidney. She has been doing a splendid job of running the horse farm and you would be wise to seek out her assistance during this time.

I am sure you have many questions, and Mr. Davidson will answer them. I look forward to visiting you in Scotland with your bride.

With much love,
Edith

Alden lowered the paper to his side and let out a loud huff. He met the solicitor's eyes and asked, "Scotland?"

Mr. Davidson tipped his head. "Yes, sir," he replied. "Your great-aunt has a thriving horse farm in Scotland."

"Yes, but it is December. The roads will be treacherous during this time of year," Alden responded.

"Lady Edith has arranged for her finest coach to take you to Scotland, at your convenience," Mr. Davidson shared.

Richard brought his head up from his letter. "Great-aunt Edith cannot be serious?" he asked, his voice rising. "She wants me to be wed before the Twelfth Night? That is a little more than a month away."

"That is correct. And Lady Edith is aware of the time restraint," Mr. Davidson said.

"It is impossible!" Richard exclaimed.

Alden folded the note. "At least you don't have to marry a chit from a small village in Scotland," he muttered.

"What of me?" Rose asked. "I am supposed to attend a house party for Christmas."

"A house party? That doesn't sound like you," Alden remarked.

Turning towards him, Rose replied, "It is at my family's behest."

Alden shook his head. What his great-aunt was asking of him- of all of them- was ridiculous. How was he supposed to find a bride in a small village of Kirkcudbright? Much less, fall in love and marry her. It was ludicrous to even think of. Great-aunt Edith was just playing a game and he refused to be part of it.

"That coach will not be necessary," Alden said. "I have no intention of going to Scotland for Christmas."

"But…" Mr. Davidson started.

Alden put his hand up, stilling the solicitor's words. "I agree with what Richard said. What our Great-aunt Edith is asking of us is impossible." He walked purposefully to the door, casting a farewell nod to his cousins. "I wish you luck, but I want nothing to do with this charade."

Leaving the office, Alden descended the steps and climbed into his waiting coach. The thought of living in Scotland, much less running a horse farm, was entirely unappealing. No, he wasn't about to sacrifice his life, his friends, or his freedom for a chance to inherit a horse farm.

As the coach rolled away from the solicitor's office, Alden's mind raced. Perhaps he was being too rash. If he inherited the horse farm, he could sell it quickly and use the proceeds to purchase land in England, which was a far more desirable location. However, there was the matter of the stipulation. He would need to marry a young woman from that village. A marriage of convenience was not ideal, but it was a price he might be willing to pay.

Alden gazed out the coach window, contemplating his next move. He would find the most beautiful young woman in the village and marry her. Hopefully, she would have a fondness for horses, making the arrangement somewhat tolerable.

The coach came to a stop in front of his familial townhouse. He waited for the footman to come around to open the door. Once he exited the coach, he approached the main door.

The butler promptly opened the door, standing aside to allow Alden entry. As he stepped into the elegant entry hall, his brother's condescending voice echoed through the space. "What did our great-aunt want with someone like you?"

Alden looked heavenward. "It is rather early for insults, is it not?"

"Is it?" his brother asked, his tone dripping with smugness. "Did Great-aunt Edith need a Latin tutor?"

"No," Alden responded curtly. "She offered me a horse farm in Scotland." He didn't bring up his Great-aunt Edith's dire health, knowing Alexander's disdain for their great-aunt. He no doubt would only delight in her circumstances.

"Scotland?" Alexander asked. "That freezing, barren wasteland?"

Despite himself, Alden felt a spark of defensiveness. "Scotland is not a wasteland," he argued.

Alexander's eyes gleamed with amusement. "Well, I suppose that is a good opportunity," he hesitated, "for someone like you."

Alden had never shared a close relationship with his brother, but time only seemed to make their relationship worse. Alexander's pretentious nature and relentless reminders of Alden's perceived inferiority gnawed at him. He wanted to prove Alexander wrong. He wanted to prove everyone wrong.

"I think I will take it," Alden said, intentionally withholding the specifics of the inheritance condition. Alexander didn't need to know everything.

Alexander placed a hand on his shoulder. "Dress warm, Brother," he mocked. "I wouldn't want you to catch a cold."

Alden stood in the entry hall, watching his brother walk away. He resolved to go to Scotland, marry and inherit the horse farm. With the money from selling it, he would prove to Alexander and everyone else that he was not merely a spare. He was worth so much more. He knew he was capable of great things, but he just needed a chance to prove himself.

Miss Elinor Sidney walked down the aisle of the stables, her gaze moving from one horse to the next with a sense of pride. Each Galloway pony under her care represented a legacy she was determined to uphold.

She stopped before a stall where Skye, a bay-colored mare, greeted her with a soft nicker. Elinor laughed. "Do you want an apple?" she asked.

Skye nickered again, seemingly in response.

Reaching into a nearby bucket, Elinor retrieved an apple and extended it towards Skye. "Here you go," she said.

Without hesitation, Skye accepted the treat eagerly.

Elinor ran her hand down the mare's neck, feeling a deep sense of gratitude for her life in moments like these. If it hadn't been for Lady Edith, she might have been relegated to a life of a governess.

Approaching her was Calen, a tall and lanky groom who had been a guiding hand since she had first arrived. He had assisted her in learning the ropes of managing a horse farm.

"How's Skye daein' today?" Calen asked, coming to a stop nearby.

Elinor dropped her hand and turned to face him. "She appears to be doing quite well," she said. "I just gave her an apple."

Calen chuckled. "Ye spoil her, Miss."

"It is hard not to," Elinor responded. "And how is your wife?"

A proud smile spread across Calen's face. "She's daein' well. She's with bairn again," Calen announced.

Elinor smiled. "That is wonderful news."

Calen's chest puffed out in pride. "I'm hopin' for a lad this time, especially since we've already got two lassies."

"There is nothing wrong with girls," Elinor countered gently.

"Aye, true enough," Calen agreed. "Though it does get a bit much now that the lassies outnumber me."

Elinor's smile grew at that thought. "I am sure you will survive," she retorted. "If you will excuse me, I should be heading back for breakfast."

Calen tipped his head. "Good day tae ye, Miss."

As she exited the stables, Elinor pulled her cloak tighter around herself. The Scottish winters were harsh, and she knew firsthand the fortitude required to endure them. The manor stood ahead, its roof dusted with a fresh layer of snow, a serene backdrop against the chilly morning.

She approached the main door and was met by Bryon, the duteous, white-haired butler, who promptly opened it for her with a courteous nod. "Good morning, Miss Sidney," he said, his words holding the kindness she was all too familiar with.

Stepping into the warm embrace of the entry hall, Elinor unclasped her cloak, feeling the thaw of the chilly outdoors. "It is rather cold this morning," she remarked, handing her cloak to Bryon.

"That is to be expected," Bryon responded as he accepted the cloak. "It is winter in Scotland."

"Has my aunt come down for breakfast yet?"

"Indeed, she has. She is in the dining room," Bryon confirmed.

"Thank you, Bryon," Elinor acknowledged gratefully before making her way towards the dining room.

Entering the dining room, she found Aunt Cecilia seated at the long, rectangular table, a stack of letters spread out in front of her. Cecilia looked up from her reading as Elinor approached, offering her a warm smile. "Good morning, Dear. I was wondering when you would join me for breakfast."

Elinor pulled out a chair and settled into it gracefully. "I just came from the stables."

"Ah, your daily ritual," her aunt said with a grin. "I do worry you will catch cold and die."

"Why must everything end in death with you?" Elinor asked, amused by her aunt's dramatic flair.

Cecilia shrugged nonchalantly. "It is the truth, is it not?"

"I am only one and twenty years old. I daresay that the cold air is refreshing," Elinor contended.

"That is only because you have young lungs. I am old and could die any minute now," her aunt declared with a flourish of her hand.

As the footman placed a plate of food before Elinor, she leaned to the side, studying her aunt's silver-haired countenance. The lines etched around Cecilia's eyes and mouth were starting to deepen, a reminder of her advancing age. Elinor felt a pang of worry but quickly brushed it aside, not wanting to dwell on such thoughts.

Cecilia held up a letter to her. "You received a letter from Lady Edith," she revealed. "Would you care to read it?"

"I would," Elinor replied eagerly. It wasn't often that she received correspondence from Lady Edith, but she always delighted in reading her letters.

Cecilia leaned forward and extended the letter. Elinor accepted the letter and unfolded the paper with anticipation. As she began to read, her eyes widened in disbelief.

"Is something the matter?" her aunt asked, concern evident in her voice.

Elinor didn't answer immediately. She dropped the letter onto the table, stunned. Finally, she spoke, her voice trembling. "Lady Edith is dying," she said, feeling an immense sadness washing over her.

Cecilia gasped. "That is awful news."

Tears flooded Elinor's eyes, and she reached for a white linen napkin to wipe them away. Lady Edith was very dear to her, and the news was devastating.

Her aunt stood up and came to sit next to her, placing a comforting hand on her shoulder. "I'm sorry, Dear. I know how much Lady Edith means to you," she said. "Did she say anything else?"

Elinor blinked back her tears and picked up the letter again. "She intends to will the horse farm to her great-nephew, Mr. Alden Dandridge, assuming he is married by the Twelfth Night."

"What if he isn't married by then?" Cecilia asked.

Lowering the letter, Elinor replied, "Then the ownership of the horse farm and manor will fall to me." Even as she said the words, she still couldn't quite believe it.

Cecilia lifted her brow. "That is rather extraordinary," she said. "What does Lady Edith say about Mr. Dandridge?"

Elinor flipped over the paper but sighed. "She said nothing about him, other than the fact that he is traveling here to inspect the horse farm."

"That doesn't tell us much then," Cecilia remarked.

"What are we to do?" Elinor asked. "If Mr. Dandridge gets married, we will be forced to leave the manor. Where will we go?"

Cecilia frowned. "We will think of something."

Elinor placed the letter onto the table, her mind racing. "I could always reach out to Mr. Treanor and ask if I can access my dowry, considering the circumstances."

"I doubt he will agree to it since your father wrote in the will that you had to be six and twenty years to access it, assuming you were still unwed," Cecilia said.

"Well, we must think of something," Elinor asserted. "I do not think I could bear going to my uncle for help. He would no doubt force me to marry that insidious man."

Cecilia gave her a knowing look. "Lord Inglewood was your guardian for many years," she said.

"Yes, but he had no issue with trying to marry me off at his first opportunity," Elinor said, attempting to keep the bitterness out of her tone. "If it wasn't for Lady Edith's generosity, I might have been forced to obtain work as a governess."

"It will work out," Cecilia said, trying to sound reassuring.

Elinor rose from her seat, her heart heavy. "I wish I shared your optimism. All I feel is dread," she said. "Lady Edith is dying, and with it, all my dreams."

"You are being quite the pessimist."

"Quite frankly, I don't know what to feel," Elinor responded, her voice tight with emotion. "I need a moment alone to think."

Just then, Bryon stepped into the room and met Elinor's gaze. "A Mr. Alden Dandridge has come to call and has requested a moment of your time."

Cecilia shoved back her chair, her expression determined. "Go greet Mr. Dandridge and I will be down in a moment. I have an idea that might help our situation."

Elinor looked at her aunt expectedly. "Which is?"

"Just trust me," Cecilia replied before she departed from the room.

Turning towards the butler, Elinor asked, "Do you have any idea what my aunt is about?"

Bryon maintained a stoic expression, but his eyes crinkled around the edges in kindness. "If I were you, I would be worried," he said lightly.

"My sentiments exactly," Elinor sighed. Her aunt was many things, but being predictable was not one of those things.

Elinor picked up the letter and gently folded it, placing it into the folds of her gown. She knew she needed to go speak to Mr. Dandridge, but a part of her wanted to send him away. However, she couldn't do that. He was Lady Edith's great-nephew and should be treated with kindness.

But this was her home. She had lived here for two years, and this horse farm was important to her. She had to fight for it.

Surely this Mr. Dandridge would be reasonable and recognize that.

Chapter Two

Alden surveyed the drawing room with a sense of satisfaction. Despite the furniture and cream-colored papered walls being slightly outdated, he knew those were minor issues he could easily remedy when he decided to sell the horse farm. The manor exceeded his expectations for a small village in Scotland, with its grand architecture and well-maintained grounds.

He turned his attention towards the windows and watched the horses grazing in the distance. The scene was idyllic. It was a picturesque landscape that would undoubtedly increase the property's value. Alden hoped the horse farm would fetch a substantial price, allowing him to reinvest in land in England, which was a far better place to live.

The long clock in the corner chimed and he sighed. What was taking this Miss Sidney so long, he thought. He didn't have the time to wait around and be idle. He had much more important tasks to deal with, such as securing a bride in this god-forsaken village.

As he turned away from the window, a dark-haired young woman entered the room. His eyes widened in surprise. She was strikingly beautiful, with fair skin, expressive eyes and high cheekbones. She was dressed in a simple gown, which only seemed to add to her allure.

She smiled, and he fought the urge to return the gesture. It would do no good to show her that she had the advantage. "Good morning," she greeted, dropping into a curtsy. "Allow me to introduce myself. I am Miss Sidney."

Alden allowed himself a small smile. "I am Mr. Alden Dandridge. It is a pleasure to meet you."

Gesturing towards the settees, Miss Sidney asked, "Would you care to sit, sir?"

"I would," Alden said as he followed Miss Sidney to the settees. He waited for her to be situated before taking his own seat.

Miss Sidney's smile faded slightly but remained polite. "How was your journey?"

"Long," Alden responded. "I traveled all the way from London, and the roads were rather treacherous." He didn't want to waste his time with pleasantries, but he didn't want to offend Miss Sidney either.

"I am sorry to hear that," Miss Sidney said.

Alden settled back in his seat. "I came straightaway after I met with my Great-aunt Edith's solicitor," he shared. "Were you aware that her health is dire?"

Miss Sidney's expression grew solemn. "I received word this morning, and I must admit that I am rather devastated by the news. Were you close with your great-aunt?"

"Not particularly," Alden admitted, not wishing to dwell on such matters. "Did she inform you that I was to be arriving?"

"She did," Miss Sidney confirmed.

"Good, then that should save us a considerable amount of time," Alden said. "Great-aunt Edith informed me that you are running this horse farm."

"I am."

"Well, I am here to take that burden away from you. I will take over the books at once," Alden said.

Rather than look pleased, Miss Sidney grew visibly tense. "I do not consider running the horse farm to be burdensome. Has Lady Edith expressed displeasure with how I manage things?"

"No, but—"

She spoke over him. "Then I propose we continue to keep things the way they are, at least for the time being."

Alden had only just met Miss Sidney and didn't wish to fight with her. He needed her help if he wanted to marry before the Twelfth Night. "Very well, but I will familiarize myself with the books," he said.

Miss Sidney seemed pleased by his compromise. "That sounds fair enough."

A maid stepped into the drawing room with a tray in her hand. She placed the tray on a table in front of Miss Sidney and asked, "Would you care for me to pour, Miss?"

"No, thank you," Miss Sidney said. "I shall handle it."

Rather than leave the room, the maid walked over to the corner and sat down on a chair, reaching for her needlework.

Miss Sidney reached for the teapot and asked, "Would you care for a cup of tea?"

"I would," Alden replied.

Alden leaned forward to accept the cup and saucer and took a small sip of his tea. He needed to discuss a few things, and he knew they were rather delicate in nature. He cleared his throat. "I was wondering if you had another place to stay."

A bemused look came to Miss Sidney's face. "I beg your pardon?"

"Well, now that I am here, it is only befitting if I stay in the manor," Alden replied. "It would be entirely inappropriate for you to reside with me."

"I agree, but this is my home."

"It *was* your home," Alden gently corrected. "It will soon be mine."

Miss Sidney lowered the cup and saucer to the table. "It *might* be yours soon and I have no desire to be displaced while we wait to see. Furthermore, Lady Edith informed me that you must be married to inherit. Are you engaged?"

Alden shifted uncomfortably in his seat. "No, I am not, but I hope to be soon enough."

"Are you pursuing someone?"

"Not at this time," Alden replied.

A line between Miss Sidney's brow appeared. "I'm afraid I do not understand. How are you to be engaged soon if you have no prospects?"

Alden smiled, hoping to disarm her. "I was hoping you would help with that. There must be a young woman in the village who is looking for an advantageous marriage."

Miss Sidney opened her mouth, but promptly closed it. A myriad of emotions crossed her face before she seemed to settle on one. But what it was, he could not say. Finally, she spoke. "I will help you."

"Wonderful," Alden said.

"But on one condition." She paused. "My aunt and I will continue to reside here and you will stay at a charming cottage on the far side of the property in the woodlands."

Alden nodded. "That is more than fair."

"Thank you," Miss Sidney said.

A figure covered in a white sheet with eyeholes cut out entered the room and sat silently by the window. Alden glanced questioningly at Miss Sidney, who seemed unperturbed. "That is my aunt, Mrs. Cecilia Hardy," she explained.

He lowered his voice, so not to be overheard. "What is she doing?"

Miss Sidney shrugged. "Who knows, but it is best to pretend that she is not here," she said.

"Is your aunt mad?"

Rather than answer his question directly, she replied, "Are we all not a wee bit mad?"

No.

What an absurd response.

Rising, Miss Sidney said, "I will inform our butler, Bryon, that you will be staying at the cottage for the foreseeable future."

Alden stood, placing his teacup on the table. "I shall accompany you."

"Wonderful," Miss Sidney murmured, but there was a terseness to her words.

With a glance at Mrs. Hardy, Alden asked, "Will your aunt be all right?"

"Of course, but it is best to pretend that she isn't here and we don't acknowledge her," Miss Sidney replied. "She comes and goes as she pleases."

"Under the disguise of a sheet?" Alden inquired.

Miss Sidney bobbed her head. "It is much easier that way," she replied before she started to walk towards the door.

Alden followed close behind and they stepped into the entry hall. The white-haired butler's eyes softened when he saw Miss Sidney approach.

Miss Sidney came to a stop in front of Bryon. "Will you ensure the cottage in the woodlands is prepared for Mr. Dandridge?"

Bryon's brow lifted. "The cottage?"

"Yes, the charming cottage on the far side of the property," Miss Sidney said. "The one Mr. Warren used when he worked for us. I am sure that it will be to Mr. Dandridge's liking."

"Yes, Miss," Bryon said, looking hesitant. "I shall see to the preparations at once, but it might take some time to air it out. It has been vacant for some time now."

"Take all the time you need, Bryon," Miss Sidney said,

turning to face Alden. "That shall give us plenty of time to take a tour of the horse farm."

"Now?" Alden asked, feeling the chill of the Scottish weather. He preferred to stay indoors, where it was warm. His stomach growled, reminding him he had skipped breakfast. "I would prefer to eat breakfast, if that wouldn't be too much trouble."

"No trouble at all," Miss Sidney said as she led him towards the dining room. "If you tell me what you would like to eat, I will gladly tell the cook."

"I will be happy with whatever the cook sees fit to feed me," Alden remarked.

Miss Sidney tipped her head. "Very well," she said, stopping by a door. "Wait here and I will be back shortly."

Alden entered the dining room and took a seat at the long, rectangular table. He wondered why Miss Sidney hadn't relayed the message to one of her footmen standing watch but decided it wasn't his place to question her methods.

The dining room's dark red papered walls and thick drapes gave the room a warm, cozy feel, a stark contrast to the cold outside. As he waited for breakfast, he contemplated the tasks ahead and wondered how quickly he could get married and leave this place.

As Elinor walked away from the dining room, Bryon approached her with a concerned look on his features. "A word, Miss."

Elinor waved him over to the parlor door and stepped inside, knowing this was a conversation that would be best in private. "I must assume you wish to speak about the cottage."

"Yes, I am not sure the cottage is habitable," Bryon said. "It has been well over a year since anyone has stayed there."

"Just do the best that you can," Elinor responded.

Bryon frowned. "Are you not worried that Mr. Dandridge will be upset with you when he sees the state of the cottage?"

Elinor waved her hand dismissively. "It is far preferable to him staying here at the manor. With any luck, he will have his valet pack his trunks and they will leave before the evening is out."

"What of Lady Edith?" Bryon asked. "Will she not be disappointed in the poor treatment you are giving to Mr. Dandridge?"

With a glance at the doorway, Elinor shared, "If Mr. Dandridge fails to marry by the Twelfth Night, the manor and horse farm will belong to me."

Bryon's eyes shone with understanding. "This is a dangerous game you are playing, Miss, but I will support you."

"Thank you," Elinor said.

"Now, dare I ask why your aunt has a sheet over her head?" Bryon asked with a smile tugging at his lips.

Elinor shrugged. "I am not quite sure about that, but I am sure she has a reason," she responded.

Bryon tipped his head. "Very well," he said. "I will ensure the cottage gets a thorough cleaning at once."

After the butler departed from the parlor, Elinor headed down the servants' stairs to see their cook. She arrived in the warm kitchen and watched as Mrs. Beaton hurried about, wiping her hands on an apron that hung around her neck.

"Good morning," Elinor greeted.

The tall, thin cook stopped what she was doing and smiled. "Guid mornin' tae ye, Miss," she said. "What brings ye by the kitchen today?"

"Lady Edith's great-nephew, Mr. Dandridge, has arrived and is requesting breakfast," Elinor responded.

Mrs. Beaton lifted her brow. "And ye had tae come doon here yerself tae tell me?" she asked.

Elinor sat down at a round table that the servants used to

eat their meals. "I saw no reason to spend additional time with Mr. Dandridge."

"Why's that, then?"

An image of the handsome Mr. Dandridge came to her mind. Tall, dark-haired, and with a strong jaw. The way he smiled at her made it evident that he was aware of his good looks and used it to his advantage. But she was not one to fall for a handsome face. She was far too practical for that.

Elinor placed her elbow on the table and rested her chin on her hand. "He is rather cocky for his own good."

Mrs. Beaton gave her a knowing look. "By the sound of it, Mr. Dandridge must be a rather dashin' lad, aye."

"Dashing? No, far from it," Elinor lied. "He is tolerable, I suppose."

"Ye cannae fool me, Miss," Mrs. Beaton said.

Elinor did not want to be having this conversation with anyone. Her heart had been shuttered away, and she saw no reason to ever open herself up to heartache. She had come to the realization that she would most likely become a spinster. Which was fine by her. She didn't need a man lording over her.

Mrs. Beaton must have taken pity on her because she didn't press her. Rather, she said, "I will send up a tray tae the dining room for Mr. Dandridge."

"Thank you," Elinor responded before rising. "I should be upstairs anyways. I have loads of work to do."

"Ye work too hard," Mrs. Beaton said with a knowing look. "Why not slow doon and enjoy life?"

"I will rest when I am able," Elinor stated.

Mrs. Beaton shook her head. "One day ye'll heed my advice."

Just then, her aunt stepped into the kitchen, the sheet draped over her arm. "I have an idea for supper."

Elinor grinned. "Dare I ask why you had a sheet over year head earlier?"

Cecilia laughed. "I was a ghost."

"I think that was lost in translation," Elinor retorted. "Why, pray tell, did you decide to wear a sheet over your head?"

"It was the only thing I came up with, and I do think it worked spectacularly," Cecilia said. "No sane gentleman would force a madwoman to leave her place of residence."

The smile dimmed from Elinor's lips. "My uncle would."

"Yes, well, Lord Inglewood was a special kind of man. Let's not speak of him again," Cecilia said. "Now, back to my ideas for supper."

Elinor took a step back. "I think this is my cue to leave. I would hate to spoil the surprise that you have for Mr. Dandridge."

She turned and headed up the stairs towards the main level. Once she arrived, she walked down the corridor and glanced into the dining room. She saw Mr. Dandridge was sitting at the table and she felt some guilt at leaving him alone.

Why should she care? If she had her way, Mr. Dandridge would leave at once and she would never have to see him again. But could she treat Lady Edith's great-nephew so distastefully, especially since the woman had given her so much?

Elinor resisted the urge to groan, knowing she couldn't leave him alone. She stepped into the dining room and met Mr. Dandridge's gaze. "Your breakfast will be up shortly," she informed him.

"Would you care to join me?" Mr. Dandridge asked.

No.

She would rather be doing anything else.

Elinor mustered a smile to her lips. "I would be delighted," she said, hoping she sounded somewhat convincing.

Mr. Dandridge rose and pulled out a chair for her. She sat in the proffered chair and tried to appear unaffected when Mr. Dandridge returned to his seat. Why was she having such an unexpected- and unwanted- reaction to a man that she hardly knew?

Settling into his seat, Mr. Dandridge said, "I hardly know anything about you, but it is evident that my Great-aunt Edith trusts you very much."

"Lady Edith has been nothing but kind to me," Elinor said. "I am most grateful that she had faith in me to run her horse farm."

"I must assume that you love horses," Mr. Dandridge remarked.

A bright, genuine smile came to Elinor's lips. "I adore horses. My mother once said that I used to pretend that I was a horse, even when guests were around."

Mr. Dandridge chuckled. "I can only imagine how much that pleased your parents."

"This horse farm is known for the breeding of our Galloway ponies," Elinor explained. "They are an exceptionally fine-looking horse, have a wide, deep chest, and have a tendency to pace rather than trot."

"That is not a common horse in England, which is where I assume you are from," Mr. Dandridge said.

"It is true. I am from Kendal, but I no longer consider that home, not since my parents died," Elinor responded.

Mr. Dandridge eyed her curiously. "May I ask when they died?" he asked gently.

Tears pricked at the backs of her eyes, but Elinor blinked them back. "Three years ago," she replied.

"I see," Mr. Dandridge said. "I apologize for broaching such a sensitive subject. If it helps, my parents are both alive, and I fear that they might drive me mad."

She appreciated what Mr. Dandridge was attempting to do, but she didn't see much humor in it. She decided to change the topic to something much safer. "Where do you hail from?"

"Sussex," Mr. Dandridge responded.

"I have heard it is quite beautiful in Sussex," Elinor said, attempting to make conversation. She didn't truly care where he was from. She just wanted him to leave.

Mr. Dandridge nodded. "It is."

A silence descended over them, and it was interrupted by the arrival of a servant with a tray in her hand.

"Ah, your breakfast," Elinor said, rising. "I should go and let you eat in peace."

Mr. Dandridge placed his hand out, stilling her. "I would prefer if you stayed. I am not used to eating in silence."

Elinor returned to her seat. "I am," she admitted.

"What of your aunt?" Mr. Dandridge asked as he picked up his fork and knife.

"Aunt Cecilia dines with me, but when I lived with my uncle, it was quite different," Elinor shared. "He tended to eat at the club for his meals."

Mr. Dandridge started eating, a thoughtful look on his face. "May I ask how old you are?"

"I am one and twenty years old," Elinor replied.

"And you are not married?"

Elinor's back went rigid. "That is hardly a question you should ask, sir," she said curtly. "Besides, I could ask you the same thing."

Mr. Dandridge smiled, no doubt in an attempt to flatter her. "I meant no disrespect. You are a beautiful young woman and I imagine you could have your pick of suitors."

She wasn't fooled by Mr. Dandridge's remark, nor was he the only gentleman that thought that way. She was still too young to be considered a spinster, but she had no interest in marrying, despite the many men who had attempted to be her suitor over the years.

"If you must know, I devote all my time to this horse farm to ensure it is profitable," Elinor said. "I do not want to let Lady Edith down."

"I had my solicitor look into this horse farm and discovered it was quite profitable. You must be doing something right."

Elinor watched as Mr. Dandridge ate his breakfast and she had no desire to spend time with him. If she got to know him, and he turned out to be a decent man, she would feel bad that she was plotting for him to fail at securing a bride.

She stood up. "I have much work that I need to see to. If you need me, I will be in the study, which is in the rear of the manor."

Mr. Dandridge had risen with her. "Thank you, Miss Sidney… for everything."

"Do not thank me yet," Elinor said before she walked over to the door. "Enjoy your breakfast, Mr. Dandridge."

He tipped his head. "I will be seeing you soon for the tour of the horse farm."

"I will be looking forward to it," Elinor said. Which was a lie. This was her horse farm, and she would fight to keep it that way.

Chapter Three

Alden sat at the dining table, wondering if Miss Sidney was a solution to all of his problems. She was not only beautiful but also passionate about horses. Marrying her could satisfy his great-aunt's conditions for inheriting the horse farm. Now, he just had to charm her, a task he felt confident in, especially since he was well-aware of the effect he had on women. However, he prided himself on not being a rake. Unlike his brother, he treated women with respect.

Rising from his chair, he strode into the corridor, where he saw Mrs. Hardy, still draped in a sheet, hurrying past him. He shook his head at the sight. He had never met anyone who insisted on wearing a sheet over their head. It was peculiar, but it mattered little. His focus was on marriage and leaving this miserable country as soon as possible.

With purposeful strides, he headed to the study in the rear of the manor. Inside, he found Miss Sidney hunched over the ledgers at the desk. In a soft voice, careful to not startle her, Alden said, "Hello, again."

Miss Sidney's head snapped up, and her eyes flashed with what seemed like annoyance. But that was impossible. Wasn't it?

He smiled, knowing how his smile affected women. "I was hoping for that tour now," he said.

To his surprise, his smile seemed to have no effect on her. "Very well," she responded, closing the ledger and rising from her chair.

Her lackluster response only strengthened Alden's resolve. He would win her over. That, he was sure of.

Miss Sidney came around the desk and smiled. Although, it didn't reach her eyes. He wondered what it would take to make her truly smile.

Offering his arm, he asked, "Shall we?"

For a moment, he feared she might refuse, but then she placed her hand on his arm, and he led her from the room. In the entry hall, she dropped her hand and stepped away. "Allow me to collect my cloak."

As if on cue, the butler arrived with a black cloak. "Allow me, Miss Sidney," he said, draping it over her shoulders.

Miss Sidney tightened the strings on the cloak before turning back towards Alden. "If you have no objections, I would like to start the tour at the stables."

"I have none."

"Wonderful," she murmured.

Alden did not like this. Not one bit. He had never had to work so hard to earn a woman's favor before. It almost seemed that Miss Sidney was immune from his charms. If that was the case, this did not bode well for him.

The butler opened the door, letting in the chilly weather. Miss Sidney stepped out without bothering to wait for him.

He caught up with her on the path as he tightened his own coat around him. As they walked the short distance towards the large stables, Alden decided the silence had gone on long enough. "It is rather cold here in Scotland." Did he truly have to resort to talking about the weather?

"Is it?" Miss Sidney asked. "I hardly notice."

"You hardly notice the freezing weather?" he asked, noting her pink cheeks.

She glanced at him. "I find it refreshing."

"That is not the word I would call it," Alden muttered.

Miss Sidney came to a stop and turned to face him. "If it is too cold for you, we can return to the manor."

Now Alden suspected that Miss Sidney didn't wish to spend any time with him. "No, that won't be necessary."

Her expression hinted at disappointment. "Then, shall we?" she asked, continuing down the path.

Finding himself curious, Alden asked, "How is it that you seem to enjoy this cold weather?"

Miss Sidney grew silent, her eyes growing reflective. "To me, it reminds me that I am free," she admitted.

"Free from what?"

Keeping her gaze straight ahead, she replied, "From my uncle. He was my guardian after my parents died, but I was merely a burden to him."

Alden could hear the pain in her words, and knew there was more to the story, but he didn't wish to pry. Not yet. He decided to try to change subjects and lighten the mood. "How long have you run the horse farm?"

"For two years now," Miss Sidney replied promptly, offering no additional information.

He glanced up at the sky, wondering what he could say to get Miss Sidney to open up to him. A thought occurred to him. "Your butler, Bryon, is it?" he asked.

She nodded.

"You seem rather fond of him."

That got a smile out of Miss Sidney. "I am," she confirmed. "He was the butler at my parents' country estate. Lady Edith was gracious enough to hire him on as the butler here, despite most of her servants being Scottish."

"Does that bother you?"

"Not at all," Miss Sidney replied. "At first, I had a hard time understanding some of them, but now I can blether jist like 'em."

Alden chuckled. "That is impressive."

"I am sure my old governess would disagree with you," Miss Sidney said, a smile playing on her lips.

"So, your parents had a country estate?" Alden asked, trying to pry gently into Miss Sidney's past.

Miss Sidney's smile faded, and her eyes took on a distant look. "They did, but it went to my uncle when they passed away."

"I'm sorry," he said softly, unsure of what else to say.

With a dismissive wave of her hand, Miss Sidney responded, "It is just the way things are. I am unable to change it so there is no point in dwelling on it. Life moves on."

They arrived at the stables, and Alden moved to open the door. As they stepped inside, the overwhelming smell of manure and hay assaulted his senses.

Miss Sidney acknowledged the grooms with a polite nod, and they returned the gesture before resuming their work.

As they started walking down the aisle, Miss Sidney began to speak with a note of pride in her voice. "As I said before, these are Galloway ponies and are magnificent creatures. An interesting fact is that Shakespeare mentioned these horses as "Galloway nags" in Henry IV, Part two."

"You enjoy Shakespeare?"

"I do," Miss Sidney said. "My mother instilled her love of Shakespeare in me from a young age. We used to read his plays together."

Alden grinned. "'What's in a name'?" he asked, testing her knowledge.

"'A rose by any other name would smell as sweet,'" Miss Sidney finished effortlessly. "I do so love *Romeo and Juliet*."

"I suspected as much since most women do."

Miss Sidney stopped by a bay-colored horse and reached

up to pet its neck with a gentle touch. "This is Skye," she said fondly. "Do not tell the other horses, but she is my favorite."

Skye nickered in response, nudging Miss Sidney's hand.

She laughed. "That is Skye's way of asking for an apple." She reached down to a bucket and pulled out an apple, holding it out as the horse eagerly gobbled up the treat.

Miss Sidney moved the hair out of Skye's eyes before sharing, "Galloway ponies may be small, but they are very hardy and active. They are much larger than the ponies of Wales and are highly desired for their size and temperament. They make great horses for children because of their gentle nature."

Alden could hear the affection in her voice. "You care greatly for these horses," he remarked.

"How can I not?" Miss Sidney asked, her eyes softening as she looked at Skye. "Unfortunately, many people are starting to crossbreed these horses, which is why their numbers are dwindling. It is disheartening."

"That is common to crossbreed," Alden noted, trying to sound understanding.

Miss Sidney offered him a weak smile. "It is, but that doesn't mean I have to like it," she replied. "Farmers want a horse of greater weight, better adapted to the draught, especially in Scotland. It is practical, but it dilutes the unique qualities of these ponies."

Alden reached out and petted Skye. "You must be doing something right since this horse farm is very profitable."

"I hope that is always the case," she said. "My father owned a horse farm, and he taught me everything he knew."

He turned to face her. "What horses did he breed?"

"Cleveland Bay horses," Miss Sidney said. "My father's horse farm was much smaller in size than this one, but he enjoyed it. Some might even consider it a hobby, considering he was busy with his other responsibilities."

"Cleveland Bays are very different from Galloway ponies," Alden remarked.

Miss Sidney bobbed her head. "They are, but both are remarkable in their own right. Cleveland Bays are powerful and versatile. They are excellent for both work and riding."

"If you could choose, which breed do you like the best?" Alden asked, finding himself curious about her preference.

A thoughtful look crossed Miss Sidney's face. "That is like asking a mother who her favorite child is," she replied. "Each breed has its own strengths and charm. It is impossible to choose, at least for me."

Miss Sidney continued walking down the aisle, sharing additional facts about Galloway ponies. As interesting as that was, Alden found that he was far more curious in knowing more about the beautiful- and alluring- Miss Sidney.

After Elinor showed the stables to Mr. Dandridge, she led him outside to the pasture to admire the Galloway ponies. She had to admit that he wasn't awful, but she needed to be careful to not let her guard down. She wasn't about to lose this horse farm to a man who so clearly did not even deserve it. He hardly seemed interested in the horses.

She came to a stop at the fence and placed her hand on the top rail, watching the horses graze lazily. This was a scene that she could never get tired of.

Mr. Dandridge came to stand next to her and glanced up at the cloudy sky. "Should we go back inside? It looks as if it is going to snow."

"A little snow won't hurt anyone," Elinor said lightly. "But if you insist." She was cold but didn't dare admit that, especially not to Mr. Dandridge.

As they started walking towards the manor, Mr. Dandridge asked, "Have you taken some time to consider potential brides for me from the village?"

"Indeed, I have," she said. "I can think of three women that would be perfectly suited for you."

Mr. Dandridge looked at her curiously. "And you do not think they will be opposed to a marriage of convenience?"

She shook her head. "No, I do not think that will be an issue. In fact, I think they would welcome such an arrangement."

"Wonderful," he replied. "When can I meet them?"

Tightening the cloak against her, Elinor replied, "We can call on Mrs. Gwendolyn MacBain tomorrow. She is a widow and is the great-granddaughter of a Scottish earl."

"Is she beautiful?"

"Yes," Elinor replied. "But are you sure that is the most important thing you should be focusing on?"

Mr. Dandridge clasped his arms behind his back. "What else is important?"

"My mother always told me that I should be brave and fierce," Elinor said. "And to be real, in a world full of fake."

"That is easy for you to say since you are beautiful," Mr. Dandridge remarked with a flirtatious grin.

Elinor rolled her eyes. "You can put away your flattery arsenal, sir. I am not interested in flattery."

"What are you interested in?"

"The truth," she declared.

Mr. Dandridge tipped his head in acknowledgement. "If that is the case, would a young woman like you be interested in a marriage of convenience?"

Elinor frowned. "No, I would not," she said. "If I was mad enough to ever wed, I would do so only for love."

"You must know that love is rare, especially in marriages."

"But it is not impossible," Elinor responded. "I know so because my father and mother loved one another."

Mr. Dandridge sighed. "My parents hold mutual toleration for one another. We even occasionally dine with each other for dinner."

"Don't you want more than what your parents had?" Elinor asked.

"I'm afraid I do not have that luxury," Mr. Dandridge admitted. "I am the younger son, the spare. I have to work harder to just prove myself."

Elinor nodded in understanding. "I understand that, considering I am a woman running a horse farm. People are just waiting for me to fail."

"And how do you keep out the naysayers?"

"I make sure my voice is louder than theirs," Elinor replied. "If I gave up every time someone told me I wasn't capable, I would never have been able to accomplish what I have."

Mr. Dandridge unclasped his arms and dropped them to his sides. "My brother is my biggest critic. He tells me that I am destined to forever be in his shadow."

"It sounds like he is afraid of what you could become," Elinor mused.

"I don't know if that is to be true."

Elinor turned towards him. "Why would he spend so much time tearing you down if he isn't worried that it is *he* who might fail?"

Mr. Dandridge huffed. "But he is the heir to an earldom," he said. "Whereas, I only have a small inheritance from my grandmother and hopefully this horse farm."

"Men in powerful positions can still feel threatened by their own insecurities," she reasoned.

A guarded look came to Mr. Dandridge's expression, and it was evident that she had pushed him too far with her remarks. "I would prefer if we talked about you," he said.

That was the last thing that Elinor wanted to talk about with a practical stranger. "We could always walk back to the manor in silence. I do enjoy a good quiet walk."

Mr. Dandridge chuckled. "Why are you so sure you would be in a loveless marriage if things were different?"

Elinor should have known it wouldn't be that easy. "My uncle wanted me to marry someone that was much older than me so I could bear him sons."

"That is not uncommon for young women in high Society," Mr. Dandridge remarked.

"Yes, but the man was almost the age of my grandfather," Elinor quickly replied. "In fact, he was good friends with my grandfather when they were younger."

"Oh, I see," Mr. Dandridge murmured.

Elinor worked hard to keep the bitterness out of her voice. "I pretended to go along with it until I arrived at the chapel. Once my uncle went to claim his seat, I snuck out the back and ran."

"You ran?"

"As far as I could, which was rather difficult in slippers," Elinor replied. "I had some pin money tucked away so I was able to eventually convince a hackney driver to take me to Lady Edith's townhouse. I knew that she wouldn't turn me over to my uncle."

Mr. Dandridge lifted his brow. "My great-aunt protected you?"

"She did, despite my uncle threatening to sue her for her interference," Elinor shared. "That is how I ended up here. When I look around these fields, I feel safe, knowing my uncle has no idea of where I am."

"Then why not marry and have the protection of your husband's name?"

Elinor huffed. "Again, I only wish to marry for love."

"But is it not enough for two people to enjoy one another's company?" Mr. Dandridge pressed.

"It is not that simple."

Mr. Dandridge came to a stop and gently turned her to face him. "And I contend that it is."

"Then by your logic, I could marry my butler," she said. "I enjoy his company."

"Be serious."

Elinor stood her ground. "I am," she replied. "Perhaps I will marry a groom. They like horses so we would have something to talk about."

Mr. Dandridge glanced heavenward. "You are not taking this seriously."

"You say it is simple, but I just proved you wrong," Elinor said. "There are many things that go into a good match."

He put his hands up in defeat. "Fine. I will admit the process to secure a spouse is a little more difficult than just enjoying one another's company, especially for people in high Society."

"Thank you," she said as she continued to walk up the path.

Mr. Dandridge easily matched her stride. "Do you often have to be right?"

"I do, but it comes so naturally to me," Elinor quipped.

He smiled. "I am a smart enough man to not argue with that," he said.

As they approached the main door, the door opened and the butler stood to the side to grant them entry.

Elinor removed her cloak and extended it towards the butler. "If you will excuse me, I have work that I must do."

"Can I assist you in any way?" Mr. Dandridge asked.

"There is no need."

Mr. Dandridge took a step closer to her. "I insist."

She had no desire to have Mr. Dandridge and his handsome face underfoot for the rest of the day. But what could she say to get him to change his mind? She had an idea. "Do you not wish to get settled at the cottage before dinner?"

Apparently, that worked because Mr. Dandridge said, "I suppose I should."

"Good," Elinor replied. "I shall see you at supper." And hopefully not a moment before. She just wanted to be alone.

Mr. Dandridge bowed. "Until later, Miss Sidney."

The butler gestured towards the door. "The coach to take you to the cottage will be here any moment, sir."

Elinor dropped into a curtsy. "Good day, Mr. Dandridge."

And with that, she walked away, not bothering to spare Mr. Dandridge another glance.

Chapter Four

Alden exited the coach and stared at the dilapidated, two-level, thatched-roof cottage. The structure looked like it had seen better days, with its weathered walls and sagging roof. Surely, this could not be the charming cottage Miss Sidney had described. Perhaps the interior was better maintained than the exterior, he thought, hoping for a pleasant surprise.

As he walked towards the door, he noticed a lone footman following him. He turned towards the footman and asked, "Are you sure we are at the right cottage?"

"This is the only cottage in the woodlands," the footman replied with a grimace.

"Are there any other cottages on the property?"

The footman nodded. "Yes, there is one, and it is in much better shape than this cottage," he revealed. "Furthermore, it is closer to the manor."

Alden frowned. Why hadn't Miss Sidney sent him there? Why did she relegate him to the woodlands? Did she think he needed privacy? Or was this some sort of test?

Unsure of what to think, Alden opened the door, which creaked ominously. He stepped inside, and the sound of his boots on the worn floorboards echoed through the cottage. A rickety-looking staircase ran along the side wall, appearing ready to collapse under the slightest pressure.

His short, thin valet, Hastings, stood by the hearth where a crackling fire filled the small space with warmth and light.

Hastings stepped forward to collect his great coat. "Come, warm yourself by the fire," he encouraged, his tone suggesting he was trying to make the best of a bad situation.

Alden stepped closer to the hearth and put his hands out to warm them. "Please say that my bedchamber is in better condition than the rest of the cottage."

"You do have a feather mattress, but I did have to request one from the butler," Hastings said. "He seemed reluctant to have one brought out here, but I insisted that you require that basic luxury."

He glanced up and noticed trickles of light coming through the roof. "I see that the roof is in disrepair."

"Among other things," Hastings muttered under his breath.

Alden dropped down onto the brown leather chair that groaned under his weight. "We only need to reside here until I convince Miss Sidney to marry me."

Hastings moved to stand by him, his expression a mix of concern and skepticism. "You intend to marry Miss Sidney?"

He shrugged. "I figure she is as good as any, and she is remarkably beautiful."

"Have you considered that she doesn't like you?" Hastings asked. "I merely say such a thing because she is relegating you to a cottage that should be abandoned."

"It isn't that bad," Alden attempted.

Hastings looked at him with disbelief. "Not one of your father's tenants live in such squalor."

"But this is Scotland," Alden argued. "Besides, you seem to forget that women adore me. In a short time, I will have Miss Sidney eating out of the palm of my hand."

"I wish I had your confidence," Hastings said.

Alden had to admit that it surprised him that Miss Sidney had been able to resist his advances. But he would play her game… for now. If she thought he would come crawling back to the manor to complain about the state of the cottage, she was sorely mistaken. He may be a gentleman, but he used to spend time at their hunting lodge, deep in the woodlands by his country estate. He would even trap his own food and prepare it. This cottage did not scare him, but rather strengthened his resolve to win Miss Sidney over.

There was only one thing that scared him and that was spiders. It had been that way since he was young. It was an impractical fear, but a fear, nonetheless. His brother had used this fear to his advantage and would often sneak spiders into his bedchamber.

Rising, Alden asked, "Where is my bedchamber?"

Hastings pointed upward. "It is on the next level."

"I think I would like to rest before supper, considering we were up at such an early hour this morning," Alden said.

"Would you like me to assist you in undressing?"

Alden shook his head. "No, that won't be necessary," he said before he walked over to the stairs.

As he placed his foot on the step, the wood creaked and dipped slightly under his weight. That is not good, he thought. He carefully ascended the stairs, wincing at each groan of the wood, and arrived at his bedchamber. He had just started removing his cravat when he heard a distinctive thud.

Alden turned back towards the door. "Hastings?"

When his valet didn't respond, he draped his cravat over his neck and headed towards the bed. He had just moved to pull back the blanket, hoping to find some semblance of comfort in this dismal place. As he moved the blanket, he noticed a flicker of movement from under the bed out of the corner of his eye.

He crouched down and his eyes widened in shock. There,

lurking in the shadows, was a giant house spider, its long, hairy legs spread out menacingly.

Jumping up, Alden ran out of his room and dashed down the stairs, his heart pounding in his chest. "There was a massive spider under my bed!" he exclaimed.

"Would you like me to remove it?" Hastings asked calmly, clearly unaware of how large the spider was.

"No, we are getting out of this cottage once and for all," Alden responded, hastily grabbing his cloak. "Pack up my trunks and return to the manor."

"Sir..." Hastings started, but Alden had already swung open the main door.

"I will inform the butler to send the coach for you at once," he stated. "And for heaven's sake, do not look under my bed."

He didn't bother to wait for his valet to respond before he charged out the door. Alden could endure most things, but sharing a space with a giant house spider was not one of them. He wouldn't do it.

With swift, determined strides, Alden exited the woodlands, the trees thinning out as he crossed the field towards the manor. He reached the entrance and flung the door open, sighing in relief as warmth enveloped him.

"Miss Sidney!" Alden shouted, his voice carrying through the hall.

A moment later, Miss Sidney appeared from a corridor, a look of curiosity and concern on her features. "What is wrong?"

Alden closed the distance between them, his anger still simmering. "How could you send me to that cottage?"

She met his gaze with a blank stare. "I don't understand," she replied. "Is it not up to your liking?"

"My liking?" he repeated, incredulous. "It should be condemned."

"It isn't that bad," she argued.

Alden raised his hands in exasperation. "There was a massive spider under my bed. My bed, Miss Sidney!"

Miss Sidney's expression softened with understanding. "That was just a house spider, and they are completely harmless."

"It didn't look harmless," Alden contended. "What if I had been in bed and it had decided to join me?"

"Spiders are important since they eat the insects…" Miss Sidney began.

Alden put his hand up, stilling her words. "I am aware of what spiders' roles are, but I refuse to stay at a cottage when I might be eaten by one."

Miss Sidney gave him a weak smile. "I'm afraid that house spiders are very common in Scotland. They enter through the chimneys and under doorways. You can't prevent them from coming inside."

"Are you not the least bit afraid of spiders?" Alden asked, his voice tinged with disbelief.

"I have grown accustomed to them," Miss Sidney admitted. "They truly mean you no harm. If you had to be afraid of something, I would be afraid of the adder. That particular snake is poisonous and is common in our area."

Alden took a step back, his eyes widening. Drats. Now he had a new fear. "I demand that you let me stay at the other cottage. The one that is closer to the manor."

Miss Sidney nodded. "Of course," she said. "That won't be an issue. I just thought you would want to enjoy the tranquility that the cottage in the woodlands provided."

"Tranquility is the least of my concerns," Alden responded.

Turning towards the butler, who had been standing nearby, Miss Sidney instructed, "Please send the coach to the cottage to collect Mr. Dandridge's trunks and deliver them to the other cottage."

Bryon tipped his head in response. "Yes, Miss Sidney," he said before hurrying off to carry out her instructions.

Miss Sidney clasped her hands in front of her and brought her gaze back to Alden. "Would you care for a cup of tea?"

"No, but I wouldn't mind sitting down," Alden replied.

Gesturing towards the drawing room, Miss Sidney suggested, "Why don't you rest before supper? Our cook has a special meal planned." She lowered her voice. "Not even I am privy to what she is going to serve, but I have no doubt that it will be delicious."

Alden suddenly felt rather silly for how he had reacted. Perhaps the spider wasn't as big of an issue as he had made it out to be. "Miss Sidney, I am sorry if I…"

"You have no reason to apologize," she interrupted, her tone gentle. "I just want you to be comfortable here since this will all be yours one day."

"Thank you," Alden said.

"Had I known you were afraid of spiders—"

He cut her off. "I am not afraid of spiders," he lied. "I only take issues with ones that are as large as a house cat."

Miss Sidney stepped forward, giving him a reassuring smile. "To ease your mind, I will direct the servants to scour the cottage where you will be residing in search of any spiders."

Alden ran a hand through his hair. "That is most thoughtful of you."

"It is the least I can do," she said. "Now, if you will excuse me, I need to get back to work. But I will see you for supper."

As Miss Sidney walked away, Alden couldn't quite believe how calm she was about the house spiders.

Once Elinor was out of sight of Mr. Dandridge, she shuddered at the thought of the giant house spider that he had described. How she loathed spiders, especially house spiders. Their long legs and plump bodies made her skin crawl. They were harmless, but their mere size always made her cringe. She would never admit it to Mr. Dandridge, but she'd had a similar reaction when she'd encountered her first house spider, jumping back with a shriek and refusing to return to her room until it was dealt with.

She arrived at her study and walked around the large mahogany desk, opening the ledger in front of her. Moments later, her aunt stepped into the room, closing the door behind her with a soft click. "I heard shouting. Is everything all right?"

"It is," Elinor confirmed. "Poor Mr. Dandridge came face to face with a house spider and he was rather upset about it."

"House spiders can grow to be rather large," her aunt mused, moving to sit in one of the chairs that faced the desk.

"That they can, but they are everywhere in Scotland," Elinor said, settling into her own chair. "It is just one of the many things I have had to get used to here."

Her aunt grinned, a twinkle in her eyes. "Can anyone get used to seeing a massive spider staring back at them?"

"No, I suppose not," Elinor responded, shaking her head. "I was half-hoping that Mr. Dandridge would give up and leave Scotland."

"I don't think it is going to be that easy."

Elinor nodded. "I agree, which is why I have selected three perfect young women to introduce Mr. Dandridge to."

Her aunt lifted her brow. "Is that so?"

"Yes, I was thinking that Mrs. Gwendolyn MacBain, Miss Isobel Fraser, and Miss Maisie Cowen would all be interested in a marriage of convenience with Mr. Dandridge."

Her aunt let out a slight huff. "You must not think very highly of Mr. Dandridge since you picked three uninteresting young women."

"It is not a matter of thinking highly of him," Elinor contended. "If he fails to marry by the Twelfth Night, then the horse farm is mine."

"I understand your reasonings but be careful. You don't want Mr. Dandridge to see what you are attempting to do," her aunt cautioned.

Elinor leaned forward in her seat. "I promise I will be careful."

"Good," her aunt said. "I would hurry down to the kitchen and eat something before we adjourn for supper."

Arching an eyebrow, Elinor asked, "Dare I ask why?"

"Mrs. Beaton is going to make a traditional Scottish meal and I do not think you will care for it," her aunt responded.

"That isn't fair. I normally enjoy Mrs. Beaton's cooking."

"Yes, but the soup this evening will be Sheep's Head Broth," her aunt said.

Elinor shrugged, trying to hide her apprehension. "That doesn't seem so bad."

Her aunt laughed. "Mrs. Beaton chose a large, fat, young sheep head from the blacksmith and soaked it for hours. Then, she removed the glassy part of the eyes and split the head with a cleaver…"

Putting her hand up to stop her aunt from speaking, Elinor said, "I am beginning to understand now."

"It sounds terrible, but it is a favorite amongst the locals in the village," her aunt shared.

"Dare I ask what is being served for the main course?" Elinor asked, her curiosity piqued.

Her aunt looked amused. "Roasted Fowl with Drappit Egg," she replied. "It is a poached egg, but it is prepared in a lamb's head. At least a lamb's head is much smaller than a sheep's."

"Yes, how wonderful," Elinor muttered.

Growing serious, her aunt reached into the folds of her

gown and pulled out a letter. "You got a letter from your uncle."

Elinor's back grew rigid as she stared at the letter. "How did he find me?" she asked, feeling only dread.

"I don't know, considering we were so careful," her aunt replied. "Would you care to read it?"

"No," came her blunt response, her tone leaving no room for argument.

Her aunt offered her a sympathetic look, her eyes softening. "Would you like me to read it, at least to see what he wants?"

"It doesn't matter," Elinor responded. "I already know what he wants, and I refuse to do it."

"Perhaps he changed his mind," her aunt suggested gently, though her expression conveyed doubt.

"My uncle is many things, but he is not one to change his mind. He is stubborn, almost to a fault," Elinor insisted.

"It seems like you and he have something in common," her aunt teased.

Elinor sighed. "I do not know how you can make jokes at a time like this," she said. "My uncle has discovered where I am. What if he comes to retrieve me himself? I don't think I could face him again."

Her aunt slipped the letter back into the folds of her gown. "He won't," she replied. "Regardless, you have reached your majority. He can't force you to do anything."

"That doesn't mean he won't keep trying," Elinor said. She knew her uncle's tenacity all too well, and the thought of him pursuing her filled her with dread.

A knock came at the door, interrupting their conversation.

Her aunt rose swiftly and walked over to the wall, where she pressed a hidden latch, revealing a narrow servants' corridor.

Once her aunt disappeared within, closing the wall behind her, Elinor ordered, "Enter."

The door creaked opened and Mr. Dandridge stepped into the room. He glanced around, a puzzled expression on his face. "I thought I heard you talking to someone."

"I was," Elinor confirmed. "I was speaking to my aunt, but she left through the servants' entrance."

Mr. Dandridge seemed satisfied by her response, but his eyes held a flicker of uncertainty. "I just want to apologize for my behavior earlier. I had no right to yell at you, considering you were only trying to help me."

Elinor felt a twinge of guilt at his words since she had been doing the opposite. "There is no need to apologize. I do think the other cottage will be much more to your liking."

He approached the desk, his steps tentative, and gestured towards the chair. "May I?" he asked.

"You may," Elinor responded, leaning back in her seat.

Mr. Dandridge sat down and turned his attention towards her. "When do you suppose I will be formally introduced to your aunt?"

"It is hard to say," Elinor said. "She is rather peculiar when it comes to meeting new people, but I shall speak to her."

A look of genuine admiration flickered in Mr. Dandridge's eyes. "You are a good person to care for your aunt in such a fashion."

Elinor let out a soft laugh. "I assure you that my aunt keeps me very entertained. I never quite know what she is going to do next, but I am most grateful for her companionship. She was the one who originally introduced me to Lady Edith. They are dear friends."

"That does not surprise me," Mr. Dandridge said in a low voice, almost as if speaking to himself.

She furrowed her brows. "Why do you say that?"

Mr. Dandridge shifted uncomfortably in his seat. "My great-aunt can be rather eccentric, and I have never had a close relationship with her."

"Yet she intends to give you her horse farm?" Elinor asked.

"I cannot say why that is, but it did come with stipulations," Mr. Dandridge admitted. "Nothing is straightforward with my Great-aunt Edith."

Elinor closed the ledger that was in front of her. "Does Lady Edith know you are seeking a marriage of convenience?"

"No, but I don't know what else she expects," Mr. Dandridge said, his frustration evident. "It is nearly impossible to fall in love in such a short time."

"I am only saying as much because Lady Edith married for love and was blissfully happy with her husband," Elinor pointed out.

Mr. Dandridge scoffed, his expression turning dismissive. "Yes, but she married a lowly merchant."

Elinor stared back at him in disbelief. "I daresay that she is the lucky one. She followed her heart and found true happiness. Can you say the same?"

He looked away, unable to meet her gaze. "People in our positions must choose duty over the dictates of our hearts."

"Is that what you truly believe?" Elinor asked.

"It is," Mr. Dandridge confirmed.

Elinor rose, smoothing down her skirts. "I disagree, most ardently," she responded, her voice firm. "If you will excuse me, I need to go speak to the cook."

Mr. Dandridge met her gaze, confusion evident in his voice. "Did I say something wrong?"

Yes.

Everything out of his mouth was wrong.

Elinor forced a polite smile to her lips. "I do believe that one's duty is to their heart."

"It is not that simple," Mr. Dandridge contended.

"I know, but it should be," Elinor responded. She came around the desk and walked towards the door.

"May I review the ledgers before supper?" Mr. Dandridge called out to her.

Elinor paused by the door, her hand resting on the handle. "Be my guest," she said before departing the study.

As she walked down the corridor, her thoughts raced, and she felt a sharp stab of disappointment. Mr. Dandridge, it seemed, was just like every other man of her acquaintance. They clung to the notion that duty was more important than following their own hearts. But she refused to marry anyone unless their hearts were involved.

Chapter Five

Alden heard the faint sound of the dinner bell as he sat in the study, reviewing the ledgers. He had to admit that the accounts were impeccable, and his respect for Miss Sidney grew with every line he read. Not only was she strikingly beautiful, but she was also extraordinarily competent with numbers.

He rose and took a moment to adjust his cravat. He had been unable to change for dinner and he hoped it wasn't a formal affair.

As he made his way towards the entry hall, he saw Miss Sidney descending the stairs, adorned in a lavender gown with a white net overlay. Her hair was elegantly piled atop her head, making her look every bit the epitome of perfection. He couldn't help but marvel at how someone so beautiful and accomplished was seemingly hidden away in Scotland.

He waited for her at the bottom step. "You look lovely, Miss Sidney," he praised.

"Thank you," Miss Sidney replied. "It isn't often that we have guests and I thought I should at least attempt to look presentable."

"I can't imagine that you don't have suitors banging down your door," Alden said with a grin.

Miss Sidney visibly tensed, her smile faltering slightly. "What did I say about flattery?" she asked, her tone suddenly more reserved.

"It is merely the truth," he countered.

"Well, do try to keep *your* truth to yourself," Miss Sidney remarked, clasping her hands in front of her. "Shall we adjourn to the dining room?"

"What of your aunt?" Alden inquired.

"She informed me that she would join us when she was able," Miss Sidney responded.

Alden found himself pleased by that unexpected news. He was rather enjoying spending time with Miss Sidney. Offering his arm, he asked, "May I escort you?"

Miss Sidney placed her hand on his and he led her into the dining room. He noticed that the table was set for them to dine at opposite ends of the long, rectangular table. Slipping her hand from his, Miss Sidney moved to sit at one end, placing her white linen napkin on her lap.

Alden took his seat, but he did not like how far Miss Sidney was from him. He preferred to admire her up close, not from afar. As he settled in, the footmen stepped forward, placing bowls of soup before them. He looked down at the soup and asked, "What is this?"

"Powsowdie," one of the footmen replied before stepping back.

Alden noticed that Miss Sidney was demurely sipping her soup so he assumed it must taste better than it looked. He picked up his spoon and dipped it into the broth, bringing it to his lips. The flavors of dried peas and barley surprised him.

"This is delicious," Alden acknowledged, raising his voice to ensure Miss Sidney heard him.

Miss Sidney gave him a questioning look. "Pardon?"

Alden raised his voice even further. "This is delicious," he shouted.

"I am so glad that you like it," Miss Sidney responded. "Not everyone would eat a soup that is prepared in a sheep's head."

Alden dropped his spoon. "I beg your pardon?" He must have misheard her.

Miss Sidney smiled. "Powsowdie is also known as Sheep's Head Broth," she explained. "The cook prepared it with sheep's trotters."

"Trotters?" Alden repeated, his voice tinged with disgust.

"Yes, trotters are the feet of the sheep," Miss Sidney revealed. "The cook wanted to prepare you a traditional Scottish meal."

Alden stared at the soup, his appetite vanishing. "And you like this?" he asked incredulously.

"Don't you?" Miss Sidney asked, a teasing glint in her eyes.

"I did before I realized what was in the broth," Alden admitted.

Miss Sidney laughed lightly. "It is common for sheep's trotters to be boiled and are used in various dishes."

Alden flicked his wrist at the footman. "Take this away," he ordered, unable to stomach any more.

Placing her spoon onto the table, Miss Sidney said, "Perhaps the next course will be more to your liking."

He dreaded his next question, but he asked it, nonetheless. "What is the next course?"

"Roasted Fowl with Drappit Egg," Miss Sidney replied.

Alden let out a relieved sigh. "As long as it is not prepared in a sheep's head, I will no doubt enjoy it."

Miss Sidney offered him a reassuring smile. "I can confirm that it is not prepared in a sheep's head."

"Good," Alden said, feeling slightly better.

"But it is prepared in a lamb's head," Miss Sidney said with a satisfied look on her face.

Alden eyed her curiously, wondering if she was just goading him. Why would Roasted Fowl be prepared in a lamb's head? Was everything in this blasted country prepared with a head of some sort?

Just as he was about to voice his incredulity, Mrs. Hardy entered the room with a white sheet draped over her head. She sat down, and a footman quickly set a place for her. The sheet now had three holes cut into it: two for her eyes and one for her mouth.

Miss Sidney continued to sip her soup, unperturbed by her aunt's peculiar behavior. Alden found this situation maddening. Perhaps it was because he was famished, having not eaten since breakfast, and now facing a traditional Scottish meal that, truth be told, frightened him a little.

He couldn't wait to get married and leave this blasted country behind.

A footman collected Miss Sidney's bowl and she wiped the sides of her mouth with the napkin. "I am sorry you didn't like your soup," she said.

What Alden wouldn't give for pea soup, a sparerib and some pudding for dessert. Perhaps if he spoke to the cook and requested something different than Scottish food.

Knowing that Miss Sidney was still waiting for a response, Alden said, "It is of little consequence."

"I spoke to Bryon, and he assured me that all the spiders at the cottage were removed," Miss Sidney said.

"All the spiders?" Alden asked, dread creeping into his voice.

Miss Sidney bobbed her head. "This is Scotland. Spiders are very common indoors during the winter. It is much warmer there."

Alden frowned. "Wonderful."

"I do believe that you will find your cottage up to snuff,"

Miss Sidney said. "The view isn't as nice as the other one, mind you, but it has recently been remodeled."

The footmen stepped forward and placed plates in front of them. Glancing down at his plate, he saw the Roasted Fowl with a poached egg, and his stomach growled. Despite his earlier reservations, he needed to eat. He picked up his fork and knife and started eating. To his pleasant surprise, the fowl was tender and moist.

They ate in a comfortable silence, but Alden noticed that Mrs. Hardy was hardly touching her food. He turned to address her. "Is the fowl not to your liking?"

No response.

Alden turned a questioning glance to Miss Sidney. "Does your aunt not speak?"

"When she is a ghost, she tends to keep to herself," Miss Sidney replied. "Just pretend as if she isn't here."

"That is rather hard to do," Alden said.

Miss Sidney placed her fork and knife down onto the plate, indicating she was done. "Ghosts can be quite peculiar about their meals," she said with a wry smile. "But I assure you, she means no harm."

Alden settled back in his seat. "This is certainly the most unique dinner I have ever attended."

"Welcome to Scotland, Mr. Dandridge. There is never a dull moment here," Miss Sidney responded.

"I am beginning to see that." He reached for his glass and said, "I must admit that I am impressed by your bookkeeping skills."

Miss Sidney leaned to the side as a footman collected her plate. "My father taught me how to balance a ledger and I suppose it stuck," she revealed.

Alden placed his glass down. "That was rather progressive of your father."

"My father encouraged my intellectual prowess," Miss

Sidney said, a hint of pride in her voice. "He never once made me feel less than for not being born a man."

"Nor should he have," Alden said, his tone firm.

Miss Sidney offered him a weak smile. "My father had no sons, and it took many years before my parents had me."

Alden pushed his plate away. "My mother did her duty. She bore an heir and a spare for my father," he said, attempting to keep the bitterness out of his voice.

"I'm sorry," Miss Sidney said.

"You said nothing wrong, Miss Sidney," he rushed to assure her. "My family is complicated and is not something that is pleasant to talk about."

Miss Sidney bobbed her head. "I understand. I try to avoid speaking of my uncle at all costs. He is not a man that I admire or wish to emulate in any way."

A footman collected his plate before another one placed a plate of pudding in front of him. Alden eyed it warily. "Dare I ask if this pudding was prepared in any head?" he inquired, raising an eyebrow.

"No, of course not," Miss Sidney responded. "Petchah is a traditional Scottish dessert."

Picking up a spoon, Alden tapped the pudding before asking, "Is it made with sheep's trotters?"

A laugh escaped Miss Sidney's lips. "Heavens, no!" she exclaimed. "It is simply pudding."

He scooped some pudding up and brought it to his lips, but Miss Sidney's next words made him pause.

"Although, I think it is only fair that you know that it is made from calves' feet," Miss Sidney shared.

Alden let out a sigh, muttering under his breath, "What is wrong with this blasted country?" He stared at the pudding, feeling only frustration. Well, he might as well at least try it, especially since he had come this far.

He took a bite, trying to pretend he wasn't chewing calves'

feet. Nope. He couldn't do it. He lowered his spoon to his plate.

Miss Sidney watched him with a sympathetic smile. "It is an acquired taste," she admitted. "Not everyone takes to Scottish traditional dishes right away."

Mrs. Hardy suddenly jumped up from her seat, her ghostly guise fluttering as she hurried out of the room.

Miss Sidney watched her aunt's hasty departure with a serene expression, but then she shoved back her chair and rose gracefully. "I do believe I shall retire for the evening," she announced.

Alden felt a stab of disappointment at that. He wasn't quite ready to say goodbye to Miss Sidney. The evening, despite its peculiarities, had been intriguing, and he found himself longing for more of her company.

He rose from his seat and bowed politely. "Good evening, Miss Sidney."

She dropped into a curtsy. "Good evening, Mr. Dandridge," she said. "When you are ready to depart for your cottage, Bryon will see to the coach being brought around front."

"Thank you," he responded, though he wished he could think of something to prolong their conversation.

As Miss Sidney walked off, Alden's mind raced. He wanted to keep her longer, to learn more about her, but he found himself at a loss for words.

Once departed from the dining room, Elinor made her way to the kitchen on the lower level. She was starving and needed some sustenance. Even she couldn't stomach what Mrs. Beaton had prepared.

She stepped into the kitchen and saw Mrs. Beaton cutting

a loaf of bread. "Come, sit," she encouraged. "I figured ye'd would be doon right about now."

Elinor went to the table and sat down. "I'm sorry, but I tried to eat the food you prepared. I'm afraid I couldn't stomach it."

Mrs. Beaton laughed heartily. "Ye'll never truly be a Scot if ye cannae eat our traditional food."

"I prefer British food," Elinor said. "Fortunately, you are an excellent cook and prepared those dishes perfectly."

"Now, ye can stop with yer flattery," Mrs. Beaton said, placing a slice of freshly baked bread on a plate. "How did Mr. Dandridge fare?"

"Not much better than me, I'm afraid," Elinor responded.

Mrs. Beaton walked the plate over to the table and set it down. "Poor man. He must be starvin'," she remarked. "I heard he acted like a *bampot* over house spiders."

Elinor shrugged. "I do not fault him for that. House spiders can grow to be rather massive, especially here in Scotland. And do not even get me started on how fast they are or how you can hear a thud when they drop down from the ceiling."

"Should I make Mr. Dandridge a typical Scottish breakfast or should we go easy on him in the mornin'?" Mrs. Beaton asked.

Her aunt stepped into the room, the white sheet draped over her arm. "I am thinking sliced haggis would be an excellent breakfast tomorrow for our guest."

Mrs. Beaton wiped her hands on the apron that hung around her neck. "Ye do realize that some folks actually enjoy haggis."

"I know, but we are trying to get Mr. Dandridge to leave, and quickly," Elinor said. "Once he realizes that Scotland is not to his liking, he will return home."

"Very well, but I will be servin' bread for breakfast, as well. I dinnae want the man tae starve," Mrs. Beaton responded.

Her aunt settled into the chair next to Elinor. "I think Mr. Dandridge is used to me in the sheet now."

"Does that mean you are going to finally take it off and converse with us?" Elinor asked.

"Perhaps, but I do think I need to up the stakes," her aunt replied. "What do you think about me playing the bagpipes?"

Elinor's brow furrowed. "You don't play the bagpipes."

"Precisely," her aunt replied with a mischievous smile. "What if I started to learn? We have a bagpipe set in the music room."

"I think that is a terrible idea," Elinor said.

Her aunt clasped her hands together. "I knew you would love it."

"No, I said it was a *terrible* idea," Elinor corrected. "Are you even listening to me?"

"I am, but I have already made up my mind. When Mr. Dandridge comes to call tomorrow, I shall impress him with my skills," her aunt said with a satisfied nod.

Elinor huffed. "You have no skills."

Her aunt feigned outrage. "I will have you know that my great-grandfather played the bagpipes."

"That doesn't mean you would be good at playing the bagpipes," Elinor remarked. "Besides, I am taking him to visit Gwendolyn tomorrow. I do say that is punishment enough for one day."

With a bob of her head, her aunt said, "You make a good point." She promptly rose. "I am going to bed. It is late and I am tired."

Elinor eyed her aunt suspiciously. "You are plotting something, aren't you?"

"It is best that you don't know," her aunt said with a wink. "Goodnight."

As her aunt hurried up the steps, Mrs. Beaton smiled and remarked, "Yer aunt is always up to somethin'," she said.

Elinor rose. "She is," she agreed. "I think I will go select a book from the library to read this evening."

"Dinnae forget yer bread," Mrs. Beaton said, gesturing to the slice still on the table.

Elinor picked up the bread and headed up the stairs. As she walked down the corridor, Mr. Dandridge stepped out of the dining room and she ran right into him, smushing her bread in the process.

Mr. Dandridge steadied her with a gentle hand. "My apologies, Miss Sidney. I wasn't watching where I was going."

"No harm done," Elinor responded, though she glanced ruefully at the squished bread in her hand. What a waste, she thought.

"Where did you get bread?" he asked, almost eagerly.

Elinor blinked, searching for words. "I... uh... went to the kitchen to thank Mrs. Beaton for the wonderful meal and she gave me a piece of bread. I always eat a piece of bread right before I go to bed."

"Then I am sorry to ruin your nightly routine," he said with a slight smile.

A footman stepped forward to take her bread, and she brushed off the breadcrumbs from her hand. "It is all right."

"Shall we go to the kitchen together to get a piece?" he offered.

"That won't be necessary," Elinor responded quickly. "I am still full from the delicious food I ate for dinner."

Mr. Dandridge nodded. "Very well. I was just about to retire for the evening, but I was hoping to speak to you about something."

Elinor mustered a smile to her lips as she pretended to appear interested in what he was about to say. "Of course. What would you care to discuss?"

He put his hands up, looking hesitant. "Why have you not started to decorate the manor for Christmas?" he asked. "I have looked, and I have not seen one decoration."

Her smile faded. "The reason is simple. I do not celebrate Christmas."

"At all?" he asked, his tone softening.

She pursed her lips, feeling the weight of her memories. "My parents died around Christmas time, and I do not like to be reminded of such things."

Mr. Dandridge's eyes held understanding. "I'm sorry. I didn't know."

"Will there be anything else?" Elinor asked, adopting a more formal tone. She didn't dare express her emotions with Mr. Dandridge. He was a stranger. How could he understand the pain she endured every Christmas season?

He took a step closer to her. "Have you considered that your servants might want to participate in the Christmas season?"

"I have not," she admitted. "And quite frankly, it is none of your concern."

"I know, but…"

She raised her voice in indignation. "I do not believe I asked for your opinion on the matter," she replied. "Furthermore, I am in charge of this horse farm for now and I will decorate the manor as I see fit."

Mr. Dandridge tipped his head and took a step back. "You are right. I assure you that I meant no offense."

Elinor could see the contrite look on his face, but she didn't care. She was angry. How dare he tell her what to do? She had run this manor- without him- and, if she had her way, she would continue to do so long after he was gone.

"Excuse me," Elinor muttered before she walked away.

Once she arrived at the entry hall, she saw her aunt was watching her with a look of concern on her face. "Are you all right?" she asked. "I heard you from down the hall."

"I am fine."

Her aunt didn't quite look convinced. "If you are sure…" Her words trailed off.

Elinor bobbed her head decisively. "I am."

"Very well," her aunt said.

With a glance over her shoulder to ensure they were alone, Elinor said, "Mr. Dandridge said the most bacon-brained thing. He said that I should consider the servants' feelings about decorating the manor for Christmas."

"He isn't wrong, my dear," her aunt responded.

Elinor reared back. "How could you say such a thing?" she asked. "Do you not miss my parents at all?"

Her aunt reached out and placed a comforting hand on her sleeve. "I miss my sister, your mother, every single day," she stated. "But they are gone, and we are not. We must go on living."

"I am not sure if I can do it," Elinor admitted.

"You are stronger than you give yourself credit for," her aunt said. "Sometimes, we must look past ourselves in order to start healing."

Elinor frowned. "And you think decorating the manor will help me heal?"

"It couldn't hurt to try," her aunt replied, dropping her hand.

Taking a step back, Elinor admitted, "I am not sure if I am ready. My mother loved Christmas and our country home would be decorated to the rafters. It was such a happy time for me."

Her aunt gave her a sympathetic look. "It still can be."

"How?" she demanded, her back growing rigid. "My mother is gone, as is my father."

"You still have me, and always will."

Elinor bobbed her head. "You are right, and I am most grateful for that," she said. "I just wish that my parents were still alive."

Her aunt smiled. "But then you would have never known what you were truly capable of. After all, your father would be so proud knowing you were running a successful horse farm on your own."

"That is true," Elinor responded.

"Life is complicated and messy, but it has a way of working out precisely the way it is supposed to," her aunt counseled.

Elinor glanced at the iron railings that ran the length of the stairs. "Perhaps it wouldn't be so bad if we put up some decorations."

"I agree," her aunt said. "Come, let us retire for bed."

As Elinor walked up the stairs, she hoped that she wasn't making a mistake. The memories of her country home being decorated for Christmas were some of her most cherished ones. But perhaps it was time to make new ones.

Chapter Six

With the morning sun streaming through the window, Alden stood in front of the mirror, adjusting his cravat with meticulous care. His valet stood a few steps back, poised to render any assistance that might be needed.

Breaking the silence, Hastings spoke up. "Is this cottage much more to your liking, sir?"

"It is," Alden replied, dropping his hands from his cravat. "I have yet to see one giant house spider, which I prefer. Greatly."

"I was told that the staff went to great lengths to ensure you were comfortable in this cottage, but dare I ask why we are not residing at the manor?" Hastings inquired.

Alden turned to face his valet. "I think it is only prudent until I convince Miss Sidney to marry me."

"And what if you can't?"

He sighed. "Then I suppose I will have to select one of the young women that Miss Sidney will introduce me to."

Hastings stepped forward and brushed off Alden's jacket. "If that is the case, what do you intend to do with Miss Sidney?"

Alden grimaced slightly. "I will have no choice but to evict her once I sell the horse farm."

"I understand."

"But let's hope it won't come to that," Alden said. "Life would be much simpler if I were to wed Miss Sidney. She is beautiful and I find her to be quite tolerable."

"Tolerable?" Hastings repeated, raising an eyebrow.

Alden shifted uncomfortably in his stance. He didn't dare admit that he found Miss Sidney to be much more than tolerable. He found her to be quite delightful and he didn't mind lingering in her presence.

A knock came at the main door, and Hastings excused himself to answer it. A few moments later, he returned to announce the coach had arrived to take Alden to the manor for breakfast.

Alden exited his bedchamber and descended the stairs. He accepted his great coat from Hastings and placed it on. Then he exited the cottage and stepped into the awaiting coach.

The coach jerked forward, covering the short distance to the manor. It gave Alden only enough time to reflect on how eager he was to see Miss Sidney. He felt bad about how they had left things between them the night before. His intention hadn't been to upset her over the Christmas decorations but rather to help her. But he had messed that up. Badly.

Once the coach came to a stop, Alden exited and hurried up the steps of the manor. The door was promptly opened by the butler, and he came to an abrupt stop in the entry hall. The servants were busy with decorating the manor with greenery of all kinds.

Alden turned to the butler with a bemused look. "What is going on?"

The butler looked at him like he was a simpleton. "We are putting up decorations for Christmas, sir."

"Yes, of course, but under whose permission?" Alden pressed.

Miss Sidney's voice came from the corridor. "Mine," she said firmly.

Alden shifted his gaze towards her. "I don't understand. I thought it was too difficult for you to see the manor decorated for Christmas."

"It is," Miss Sidney responded, stopping in front of him. "However, as you pointed out, I am not the only one who lives here."

He ran a hand through his hair. "I'm sorry. That was rather callous of me to say…"

She put her hand up, stilling his words. "You have nothing to apologize for since you were right. I was only thinking of myself."

"There is nothing wrong with that," he attempted.

Miss Sidney turned her head to watch the servants place greenery on the iron railing. "It was when I was choosing to let grief rule my life," she said. "Besides, I have to admit it is nice seeing all of this greenery inside."

"It is," Alden agreed, his eyes following hers. "And the smell is rather enchanting."

"I thought I would dread looking at the decorations, but they bring up many pleasant memories, as well," Miss Sidney said with a smile. "My mother would always decorate the manor well before Christmas Eve, despite the superstition that it was bad luck. She never believed in such things."

"Neither do I," Alden said, "but I do hope you intend to put up mistletoe."

Miss Sidney did not look amused. "I do not think mistletoe is necessary to celebrate the holiday."

"You are wrong," Alden said. "Mistletoe makes Christmas that much more entertaining. You never know who will be caught under it."

"Well, I assure you that I have no intention of standing under the mistletoe with you or anyone else for that matter," Miss Sidney stated with a tilt of her chin.

Alden laughed. "You say that now—"

She spoke over him. "I will say that *always*," she said in a firm tone. "Now, would you care for some breakfast before we call on Mrs. MacBain?"

"I would," Alden said, offering his arm. "May I escort you to the dining room?"

Miss Sidney accepted his arm and they strolled towards the dining room. Once they arrived, she dropped her arm, and he went to pull out a chair for her.

Once she was settled into her seat, Alden sat next to her and a footman stepped forward, placing plates of food in front of them.

He shifted towards Miss Sidney. "I am rather eager to meet Mrs. MacBain," he said. "Does she know that I am wife hunting?"

"Yes, I mentioned that you were looking for a wife, and quickly," Miss Sidney responded.

"Good, that will save us a considerable amount of time," Alden said, picking up his fork and knife.

Miss Sidney gave him a curious look. "I do find it fascinating that you would be so willing to enter a marriage of convenience just to inherit a horse farm."

"The horse farm is very profitable."

"It is, but what if taking a wife makes you miserable?" Miss Sidney asked. "You will be tied to her for the remainder of your days."

Alden nodded. "That is why I will need to choose wisely."

"Is that even possible in such a short time?" Miss Sidney inquired.

"Why wouldn't it be?" Alden asked. "After all, I am an excellent judge of character."

Miss Sidney didn't quite look convinced. "If you say so," she muttered, turning back to her food.

Alden leaned towards her. "You don't believe me?"

"It seems rather far-fetched to me," Miss Sidney replied.

He set his fork and knife down and turned to face her. "Besides being quite beautiful, you also have a tender heart. You care, far more than you let on. And I have seen the way you treat your servants. It is with compassion and kindness." He paused. "Tell me that I am wrong."

Emotions flittered across Miss Sidney's face, but he couldn't decipher them. Was it sadness? Disappointment? Finally, after a long moment, she spoke. "You flatter me, sir."

"It was merely the truth."

"You are wrong about me, though," Miss Sidney said. "I am not as kind as you have led yourself to believe."

Alden gave her a knowing look. "I truly doubt that, considering you are willing to help me out of the goodness of your own heart."

"Well, I… uh…" Miss Sidney's words came to an abrupt halt when an older woman with silver hair stepped into the room. "Aunt Cecilia," she shouted. Loudly. She almost seemed pleased by the interruption.

Alden rose and Mrs. Hardy waved him back down. "Take your seat, young man," she said, softening her words with a smile. "It is nice to finally see you fully and not through a white sheet."

"It is a pleasure to finally meet you," he greeted.

Mrs. Hardy sat down and he followed suit. "You must excuse me, but sometimes I feel like I need to be invisible," she said.

"I can understand that," Alden responded with a grin. "I have often wished that I was invisible around my family, especially my brother."

Miss Sidney reached for her teacup and brought it up to her lips. Her perfectly formed lips. Alden cleared his throat at his wayward thought. Where had that thought even come from? He was just trying to convince Miss Sidney to marry him, not develop feelings for her. Feelings would just complicate things. And he didn't need any further complications in his life.

As Miss Sidney returned the teacup to the saucer, she turned her gaze towards her aunt. "Will you be accompanying us to visit Mrs. MacBain?"

"Heavens, no!" Mrs. Hardy exclaimed. "I think it is best if I stay behind and work on the bagpipes."

"You play the bagpipes?" Alden asked.

Mrs. Hardy bobbed her head. "Yes," she replied. "Some people would consider me quite proficient."

Miss Sidney lifted her brow. "Who are these people?"

With a dismissive swipe of her hand, Mrs. Hardy replied, "It matters not. I will be regaling you both soon with my impressive skill."

"I can't wait," Alden responded.

"Trust me, you can," Miss Sidney muttered to him.

Mrs. Hardy gave her niece a pointed look. "Make sure you take your lady's maid with you to call upon Mrs. MacBain. I do think you will have a much more open conversation without an old lady being present."

"You are hardly old," Miss Sidney attempted.

"That is rubbish! I have one foot in the grave," Mrs. Hardy declared.

Miss Sidney turned towards him and explained, "You must forgive my aunt. She is prone to exaggeration."

"I find it delightful," Alden responded.

Mrs. Hardy beamed. "Thank you, Mr. Dandridge," she said. "I knew I liked you."

Rising, Miss Sidney remarked, "Please excuse me, but I need to retrieve a hat."

Alden rose as Miss Sidney departed from the room, his eyes lingering on the doorway. She had looked rather alluring in her pale blue gown. It had complemented her stunning blue eyes that seemed to bore into his soul, making him wonder what she saw.

Mrs. Hardy's voice reminded him that he wasn't alone. "I do hope you intend to act like a gentleman when you call upon Mrs. MacBain."

He returned to his seat. "I do."

"Good." Mrs. Hardy held up her knife. "Because I am also proficient in knives." Her words held a warning.

"Are you?" he asked, unsure of what else to say.

Mrs. Hardy lowered her knife to the table. "Not really, but I hope I got my point across."

"You did," Alden confirmed.

She nodded before she rose. "Enjoy your visit with Mrs. MacBain. Not only is she eager to get married, but she can be rather entertaining."

Alden had stood up with Mrs. Hardy and found himself curious as to what she meant by that. Isn't that what he wanted? Someone that wanted to get married, and quickly? Yes. This was a good thing.

Elinor descended the stairs with her lady's maid, Sophia, following behind her. She glanced at all the greenery on the iron railing and memories came rushing back to her. Her mother loved nothing more than to decorate their country home for Christmas. She was glad that Mr. Dandridge was brave enough to broach the subject with her.

Standing in the entry hall was Mr. Dandridge. He truly was a handsome man, but it mattered not. She had to stick to her ruse if she wanted to be the owner of the horse farm, despite the guilt she felt for her actions.

Mr. Dandridge met her gaze as she stepped onto the marble floor of the entry hall. "Miss Sidney," he greeted politely.

She returned his smile and she realized how easy it was to

do so. "Mr. Dandridge." She felt a slight fluttering in her stomach as she held his gaze. This would not do. She couldn't develop feelings for a man that she was trying to cheat out of his inheritance.

Fortunately, the butler's arrival drew her attention. "The coach is out front," he announced as he moved to open the door.

Mr. Dandridge offered his arm and she accepted it. He led her out the door and towards the awaiting coach. Once he assisted her in, he reached back and did the same for Sophia. The simple action touched Elinor's heart. Not every man of her acquaintance would be so considerate of her lady's maid.

Sophia came to sit down next to her and placed a blanket over their laps. Mr. Dandridge sat across from them and the coach jerked forward.

"It won't take too long to arrive at Mrs. MacBain's manor," Elinor said, feeling a need to break the silence.

"That is good," Mr. Dandridge said. "I must admit that the manor looks very festive."

Elinor nodded. "That it does."

With compassion in his eyes, Mr. Dandridge said, "I do hope the decorations don't bring up too many bad memories."

"That is the thing," Elinor started, "it has brought far more good memories than bad ones. I didn't realize how much I missed them until now."

Mr. Dandridge's eyes crinkled around the edges. "I am glad to hear that."

Elinor cocked her head. "Will your family miss you for Christmas?"

A dry chuckle escaped Mr. Dandridge's lips. "Good gads, no," he replied. "Last Christmas, my father spent his time with his mistress and my mother spent it with her 'gentleman friend'."

"And what of your brother?"

Mr. Dandridge shrugged. "He will no doubt spend it with a woman that he is momentarily fancied with."

Unsure of what else to say, Elinor settled on, "I'm sorry."

"I'm sorry, as well," Mr. Dandridge said. "I shouldn't have brought it up, but Christmas is not a big deal in our family. Not like it was in yours."

Elinor fingered the strings of the cloak that was tied around her neck. "My mother thought Christmas was the time for family."

"And what of your family?" he asked. "Do you not want to spend time with them for Christmas?"

She frowned. "I was disowned by most of my family after I refused to marry the person my uncle selected for me."

Mr. Dandridge gave her a look that could only be construed as sympathy. "That must have been rather difficult for you."

"It was, but I don't regret my choice," Elinor said firmly. "I knew the risks when I ran from the chapel."

"I think you are brave."

Elinor huffed. "Brave?" she repeated. "That is not what my family considered me. Selfish. Stupid. Inconsiderate. Those are the words that they used."

"Well, they would be wrong."

"Thank you, but I made my bed and now I must lie in it," Elinor said.

Mr. Dandridge smirked. "I hope it is a rather comfortable bed," he quipped.

Elinor grinned. "It is," she replied. "There is no other place that I would rather be."

"Then you made the right choice," Mr. Dandridge said. "I am only glad that you still have your aunt, Mrs. Hardy, to keep you company."

"I am rather fortunate," Elinor admitted.

Mr. Dandridge cleared his throat as he shifted in his seat.

"Have you considered what you will do once I take over the ownership of the horse farm?"

No.

Because that won't happen.

But she couldn't tell Mr. Dandridge that. "Not yet," she replied. There. At least that much was true.

Mr. Dandridge held her gaze as he replied, "You could always marry me."

Elinor's brow shot up. "I beg your pardon?"

With a glance at Sophia, Mr. Dandridge continued. "I need to marry someone, and we get along nicely. It could be the perfect solution for both of us."

"You are offering me a marriage of convenience?" she asked in disbelief.

"I am, but it would be beneficial to both of us," Mr. Dandridge said. "After all, when I sell the horse farm—"

"*What?!*" Elinor asked, cutting him off.

Mr. Dandridge bobbed his head. "I intend to take the funds of the horse farm and buy land in England."

"But your Great-aunt Edith loves this horse farm," Elinor argued.

"Yes, but once I inherit it, I can do whatever I wish with it, including sell it," Mr. Dandridge said.

Elinor felt her back grow rigid. "Have you told your Great-aunt Edith this?"

"No, but—"

She spoke over him. "How could you even consider such a thing?" she asked. "The horse farm is profitable, and you could use the income to buy more land. You don't need to sell it."

Mr. Dandridge let out a deep sigh. "I know you are attached to the horse farm, but this is just a business decision. It isn't personal."

"It feels personal," Elinor muttered.

"If we were wed, you could continue to run the horse

farm until it sells," Mr. Dandridge said. He said his words as if he were dangling a treat in front of her.

Elinor couldn't quite believe what Mr. Dandridge had revealed. How could he even consider selling the horse farm? This was her home. Her sanctuary. And he wanted to take it away from her. She couldn't let that happen. Lady Edith would be furious to know of Alden's intentions. She loved this horse farm almost as much as Lady Edith did.

"No," Elinor said.

Mr. Dandridge furrowed his brows. "No?"

Elinor pressed her lips together before saying, "I won't marry you."

"Whyever not?" Mr. Dandridge asked. "It is the perfect solution for both of us."

"It may be a solution for *you*, but not for me," Elinor said. "You seem to forget that I ran away from a marriage of convenience."

"Yes, but I would be a fair and generous husband."

Elinor shook her head. "I don't want a 'fair and generous' husband," she responded. "If I marry, it will be for love."

"Love?" Mr. Dandridge scoffed. "Not this again."

"You don't seem to believe in love, but I do," Elinor declared. "And you would be the last man I would ever consider marrying."

"Surely you can't be serious. Think of your future. What would you do once I sell the horse farm?" Mr. Dandridge pressed.

Elinor shrugged. "I don't rightly know, but I will figure it out," she said.

"All right, if you really feel that way, then I take back my offer," Mr. Dandridge responded.

"Thank you," Elinor said.

"But you are wrong to dismiss me so easily," Mr. Dandridge remarked. "Loads of women would want to marry me, given the chance."

"I have no doubt."

Mr. Dandridge glanced out the window before saying, "It is true. In London, I am considered one of the most eligible bachelors."

Elinor didn't know why Mr. Dandridge was trying to press his point. She could not care less about how many women would want to marry him. He had offered her a marriage of convenience and she refused to even entertain it. But he was still the great-nephew of Lady Edith- who she owed so much. She should at least attempt to be civil with Mr. Dandridge.

"I hope I did not offend you…" Elinor started.

Mr. Dandridge put his hand up. "You did no such thing."

"Good, because I hope we can still be… friends," she said, tripping over the last word. She needed to pretend to get along with him for the sake of the ruse. But once he failed to marry by the Twelfth Night, she would evict him. Not the other way around.

He smiled. "I would like that."

"As would I," she replied, forcing a smile to her lips.

"And in the spirit of friendship, I should note that you aren't the usual type of young woman I would be interested in," Mr. Dandridge said.

Elinor reared back slightly. "I beg your pardon?"

Mr. Dandridge's smile grew smug. "You are pretty enough to tempt me, but my interest lies elsewhere."

"What does that mean?" Elinor asked, not knowing if she should be offended or not. But she was leaning towards being offended.

"It doesn't matter, does it? After all, you were the one who turned down my offer," Mr. Dandridge responded.

"Yes, but it was for a good reason," Elinor pressed.

Their conversation came to an abrupt halt when the coach came to a stop in front of a modest manor and Mr. Dandridge moved to open the door. He stepped out and reached back to assist them. She removed her hand the moment she was on firm ground.

Elinor turned her head away from Mr. Dandridge as she considered his words. What did he mean that she wasn't the type of young woman that he usually went for? Had he been trying to get a rise out of her or was it just a passing comment? Regardless, she would not dignify his comment with a response.

Or so she thought.

She shifted her gaze towards Mr. Dandridge and said, "Just so you know, loads of gentlemen wanted to court me."

Mr. Dandridge offered her a brief smile. "If you say so," he simply said.

"No, I am in earnest," Elinor insisted. "I was largely considered the diamond of the first water in my first Season."

"I believe you," Mr. Dandridge said in a lackluster response.

Clearly, he did not believe her, which irked her even more. Now he was just trying to pacify her. What an infuriating man!

Unfortunately, before she could release her sharp tongue on him, the front door of the manor opened.

Chapter Seven

Alden was thoroughly irked. Miss Sidney hadn't even truly considered his offer before dismissing it outright. Did she think she would receive a better offer from a Scotsman in this small village? He was the son of an earl, for heaven's sake. Though he may not bear a title, he was determined to make something of himself. He had to. He refused to play second fiddle to his brother for the rest of his life.

Why couldn't Miss Sidney see that this proposal was a solution to both of their problems? He would inherit the horse farm and she would have the protection of his name. Yet, she had turned him down flat. She claimed that she wanted love, but that was ridiculous. Love was elusive, an empty promise.

As he led Miss Sidney into the manor, he noticed her rigid back and her jaw was set in determination. Why was she so upset? If anything, he should be the one feeling insulted. He had never offered for a young woman before, but his offer was hardly objectionable.

The short, stout butler stood to the side as they stepped into the entry hall, ensuring the door was closed quickly to keep the cold out. "If you will follow me to the drawing room, Mrs. MacBain is expecting you."

Miss Sidney glanced over her shoulder at her lady's maid, who was settling into a chair in the entry hall. They followed the butler into a modest drawing room with blue papered walls. There, Alden saw a beautiful blonde woman, wearing a black gown. Her hair was elegantly arranged in a chignon, and a bright smile appeared on her lips as her eyes landed on him.

Yes, she would do nicely, Alden decided.

Miss Sidney dropped her arm from his and went to create more distance between them. "Good morning, Gwendolyn," she said. "I hope we did not come too early."

Mrs. MacBain waved a dismissive hand in front of her. "Not at all. I am an early riser these days," she responded.

Turning towards him, Miss Sidney offered the introductions. "Mrs. Gwendolyn MacBain, please allow me the privilege of introducing you to Mr. Dandridge. He is the great-nephew of Lady Edith."

Mrs. MacBain's eyes lit up. "I just adore Lady Edith. She has done so much for this village, including starting a girls' school."

"I hadn't realized that she had done such a thing," Alden admitted, somewhat surprised.

"Oh, yes. Lady Edith's name is spoken with such reverence here," Mrs. MacBain shared. "I have never met a more kind, considerate woman before, and she isn't even Scottish."

Alden realized he had perhaps underestimated his great-aunt. It was evident that she was well-loved in the village and made significant contributions.

Mrs. MacBain gestured to the two camelback settees. "Shall we sit and drink some tea?" she asked.

Alden put his hand out to Miss Sidney, indicating she should go first. Once she was settled into her seat, he claimed the seat next to her, trying to ignore the faint scent of lavender that wafted off her person.

A maid entered the room carrying a tea service. She

placed it down onto the table and asked, "Would you like me to pour?"

"No, thank you," Mrs. MacBain responded. "I shall see to it."

The maid tipped her head and departed from the room.

Alden's eyes roamed over the drawing room, taking in the thick maroon drapes framing the two long windows, the mantel over the hearth adorned with small trinkets, and the clock ticking softly in the background. The room exuded a cozy, welcoming charm.

Mrs. MacBain extended him a cup of tea, her gaze curious. "How are you enjoying our quaint village?"

"It is quite nice, at least the parts that I have seen," Alden replied, accepting the cup with a polite nod. "I do wish to offer my condolences for your loss."

A weak smile crossed Mrs. MacBain's lips. "Thank you," she said softly.

"May I ask how long ago your husband died?" Alden inquired.

Mrs. MacBain adjusted the sleeves of her black gown, a somber expression on her face. "Two months and three days," she answered.

Alden's brow shot up in surprise. "Two months?"

"Yes, but I intend to remarry, and quickly," Mrs. MacBain insisted. "I do not like being a widow." She flashed him a coy smile.

He cleared his throat. "Are you not worried about the gossip that will no doubt accompany marrying so quickly after your husband died?"

"It would be preferable to remaining a widow," Mrs. MacBain said firmly.

The sound of a baby crying echoed from a distant room, and Mrs. MacBain turned her head towards the noise, a look of annoyance flashing in her eyes. "I do wish the nursemaid would keep Rowan from crying. That noise grates on my ears."

Miss Sidney gave her an understanding look. "I do believe babies cry all the time."

"Yes, but this particular baby cries incessantly!" Mrs. MacBain exclaimed. "It truly vexes me."

"It is no bother," Alden attempted to reassure her.

Mrs. MacBain's face softened. "You are very kind, sir," she said. "Dare I hope that you like children?"

Alden nodded. "I do."

Miss Sidney turned to face him and shared, "Mrs. MacBain has six children, including a newborn."

"Six children?" Alden repeated.

Mrs. MacBain grinned proudly. "Yes, and they are all girls. Little redheaded girls that will be educated right alongside my sons, assuming I am blessed with more children."

"That is admirable," Alden said. "I believe an educated young woman wields quite a lot of influence."

"My husband would have ardently disagreed with you," Mrs. MacBain remarked, a hint of bitterness in her tone. "He was of the mindset that females were useless. Fortunately, his mistress had two boys so that took some of the pressure off me."

Alden felt deucedly uncomfortable and muttered, "I'm sorry."

Mrs. MacBain shook her head. "You misunderstood me. I did not mind my husband taking a mistress. It kept his hands off me, even for a moment."

Taking a sip of his tea, Alden wasn't quite sure how to respond. Mrs. MacBain was pretty enough, but he did not think he wanted to take on the responsibility of six girls. Not that he was opposed to having children, but in due time.

Miss Sidney spoke up, addressing Mrs. MacBain. "How is your mother?" she asked.

"She is well," Mrs. MacBain said. "She moved in with me after my husband died and she loves doting on her grandchildren."

Shifting her gaze towards Alden, Miss Sidney explained, "Gwendolyn's mother was on her death bed just a few years ago, but then she made a remarkable recovery. It baffled the doctors."

"It is true," Mrs. MacBain said. "I do think my mother almost lost her will to live after my father died."

"They must have loved each other very much," Alden remarked.

Mrs. MacBain let out a bark of laughter. "No, they hated each other," she declared. "My mother had married him when she was six and ten years old and she wasn't sure how to go on without him. But there was no love lost there."

Alden glanced down at his tea, feeling awkward. "I see," he muttered.

"But enough about me," Mrs. MacBain said. "I would much rather learn more about you."

Leaning forward, Alden placed his nearly full cup and saucer onto the tray. "I am the second son of an earl…"

Mrs. MacBain interrupted him, pointing towards his teacup. "Are you going to finish that?" she asked.

"Um… yes," he replied. He didn't quite understand the urgency of finishing his tea right at this precise moment.

"It is all right if you don't," Mrs. MacBain said. "I will just pour it back into the teapot so we can use it for later."

Alden studied Mrs. MacBain, wondering if she was truly serious.

Miss Sidney handed Mrs. MacBain her teacup. "I am finished," she said.

Mrs. MacBain accepted her cup and poured it back into the teapot. "There. Waste not, want not," she declared as she placed the empty teacup down onto the tray. "Now, where were we? Oh, yes. Mr. Dandridge was telling me about himself."

"Yes, as I was saying..." Alden began.

Bringing a hand to her forehead, Mrs. MacBain interrupted again, "I am sorry, but I can't focus on anything but that incessant crying."

"It isn't so bad," Miss Sidney attempted to reassure her.

Mrs. MacBain abruptly rose, causing Alden to stand, as well. "Excuse me for a moment," she said before she exited the drawing room.

Shifting on the settee towards him, Miss Sidney asked, "What do you think about Gwendolyn?"

What did he think? He was beginning to think he wanted more than just someone who had a pretty face.

His thoughts were interrupted by Mrs. MacBain shouting, "Shut that baby up! I am trying to secure a marriage proposal from the son of an earl!"

Alden had heard enough. He didn't want to marry Mrs. MacBain. At first glance, she had seemed perfect, but he couldn't tie himself to this woman for the remainder of his days.

"Shall we go?" Alden asked, extending his arm to Miss Sidney.

Miss Sidney furrowed her brow. "Already?"

"I do not think that Mrs. MacBain and I would make a good match," Alden admitted. "I would like to meet the other young women that you mentioned."

Rising, Miss Sidney accepted his arm and they walked towards the main door.

Mrs. MacBain met them in the entry hall, a pout on her lips. "Are you leaving so soon?" she asked.

"I'm afraid so," Miss Sidney replied. "We have some urgent business at the horse farm that we need to tend to."

"Very well, but I do hope Mr. Dandridge calls upon me

again," Mrs. MacBain said as she batted her eyelashes at him. "I just had some mistletoe put up."

Not wanting to dignify her words with a response, Alden bowed. "Mrs. MacBain, it was a pleasure to meet you."

Mrs. MacBain took a step closer to him and ran her hand down his sleeve. "Miss Sidney told me that you are looking for a wife. I do hope you will consider me. I can promise that I would make you very happy."

"I shall think on it," Alden said.

Taking a step back, Mrs. MacBain turned her attention towards Miss Sidney. "Elinor," she started, "as always, it was a pleasure."

Alden led Miss Sidney out of the manor and into the awaiting coach. Once the door was closed, he said, "Please say the next young woman doesn't have any children."

Miss Sidney smiled. "*Miss* Isobel Fraser has never been married before and has no children."

"Good," Alden muttered, turning his attention towards the window. That meeting with Mrs. MacBain had been a disaster. Surely it couldn't get any worse than that.

Elinor sat in the study, her brow furrowed as she reviewed the accounts. She was doing her best to avoid Mr. Dandridge, that familiar twinge of guilt gnawing at her. She knew he would have no interest in Mrs. MacBain. But to keep this horse farm, she had to maintain the ruse.

Her aunt stepped into the room with an unusually solemn look on her face. In her hand, she held up a letter. "Your uncle has written to you again."

"Toss it into the fire," Elinor remarked without looking up.

"It is not that easy this time," her aunt said, her tone heavy with concern. "A messenger delivered the letter and has been instructed to wait for a response."

Elinor's mind was racing as she asked, "How did my uncle know where to find me? I do not think Lady Edith would have betrayed my confidences."

"She wouldn't have, but it matters not. He knows where you are and that could pose a problem for us," her aunt said as she approached the desk.

"Where is the messenger?" Elinor asked, feeling the weight of the situation settling on her shoulders.

"In the kitchen," her aunt replied.

Elinor sighed, extending her hand. "I will read the letter, but I suspect I already know what is in it."

Her aunt handed over the letter, and Elinor unfolded the piece of paper with a sense of foreboding. She read the contents quickly, her face tightening as she crumpled the paper in her hand.

"What did it say?" her aunt asked.

"My uncle has threatened to send me to an asylum if I don't marry the Duke of Mardale," Elinor said. "He claims that my behavior could only be construed as hysteria since I am refusing to marry a duke."

Her aunt lowered herself down onto a chair. "What are you going to do?"

"I don't know," Elinor replied. "I refuse to marry the Duke of Mardale. He is old enough to be my grandfather."

"I do not fault you for that, but your uncle is not one to make empty threats," her aunt pointed out.

Elinor dropped the crumpled letter onto her desk. "I do not know why my uncle entered into a contract with the aged duke. If Uncle Matthew had only asked me what I wanted, I would have told him that I wasn't interested in marrying him."

"I don't think he is interested in what you want, my dear," her aunt remarked.

Leaning back in her seat, Elinor said, "I could always leave the horse farm."

"And where would you go?"

Elinor grimaced slightly, the idea of leaving the horse farm tearing at her heart. "I could become a governess and disappear."

Her aunt gave her a knowing look. "You wouldn't be happy with that alternative," she said. "You love this horse farm."

"I do, with my whole heart. But being a governess would only be until I can access my dowry at six and twenty years," Elinor acknowledged.

"We will find another solution," her aunt said, rising. "Perhaps I will write to Lady Edith and see if she can help us."

Elinor didn't like that option. Not because she didn't think Lady Edith would help her, but because she had already done so much for her. She couldn't keep relying on the woman. She needed to find a way to solve this problem on her own.

The sound of the dinner bell echoed throughout the main level, interrupting her thoughts.

Her aunt walked over to the door. "I need to retrieve my bagpipes," she informed Elinor. "I shall meet you for supper."

Elinor's brow shot up. "Your bagpipes?"

"Yes, I am planning on serenading you both over dinner," her aunt replied. "You are welcome."

"I am not sure if 'thanking you' is what I will be doing once I hear your performance," Elinor said with a smile.

Her aunt laughed. "I have gotten much better."

"But you only just started."

"Exactly! I have nowhere to go but up," her aunt said, walking to the door. "I shall inform the messenger that you have no intention of marrying the Duke of Mardale."

Elinor rose from her seat. "Thank you. I know I am risking my uncle's ire, but I can't marry the duke."

"Nor do I blame you," her aunt said. "No doubt the duke just wants to marry you to produce an heir."

Elinor shuddered at that thought. "I recall meeting him and he smelled so awful that I grew nauseous."

"I suspect it is the medicine he uses to help his gout," her aunt said.

Once her aunt had departed from the study, Elinor smoothed down her pale yellow gown and approached the mirror. It shouldn't matter to her that she looked presentable, but it did. It irked her greatly. Why did it matter what Mr. Dandridge thought of her? It didn't. But even she knew that she couldn't believe that lie. Mr. Dandridge was far too handsome for his own good.

Elinor headed towards the entry hall and saw Mr. Dandridge. His eyes crinkled around the edges when their gazes met, a subtle sign of warmth that made her heart flutter despite herself.

She stopped a short distance from him. "Good evening, Mr. Dandridge," she said, her voice steady.

"Good evening, Miss Sidney," he responded with a slight bow. "How was your rest this afternoon?"

"I'm afraid I got distracted by the accounts," Elinor responded.

He took a step closer to her. "Your dedication to this horse farm is quite impressive."

"It is all I have," Elinor admitted. "Besides, what is not to love? The Galloway ponies are impressive creatures, and they quickly claimed my heart."

Mr. Dandridge grinned. "I do enjoy how your eyes light up when you become passionate about a subject."

"Do they?" Elinor asked, slightly surprised by his observation.

He nodded. "They light up a lot, considering you are a very passionate person," he said. "I don't meet a lot of young women that speak their minds so freely."

"Then you must not be associating with the right women," she joked.

Mr. Dandridge chuckled. "I would agree with that statement," he said. "Young women of my acquaintance tend to tell me what they think I want to hear, not their true opinions."

"That must be rather lonely."

The humor left Mr. Dandridge's face. "It is," he admitted. "I prefer honesty above all else."

Elinor felt a stab of guilt, knowing she wasn't being entirely honest with Mr. Dandridge. But she couldn't let him know that.

Mr. Dandridge took another step towards her, causing her to tilt her head to look up at him. "I know we haven't known each other long, but I do consider you a friend."

Friend.

That word echoed in her mind. She was not his friend, knowing she was hoping- and waiting- for him to fail.

Mr. Dandridge continued. "I hope it is not too presumptuous of me, but I would like for you to call me by my given name."

Elinor blinked, surprised by his request. "I have never called a gentleman by his given name before."

A smirk came to his lips. "I assure you that it isn't difficult," he said. "You just open your mouth and say 'Alden'."

"Alden?" she repeated.

Mr. Dandridge's smirk grew. "You said it correctly, but you might want to work on the delivery."

Elinor laughed. "I can do that, but it is only fair if you call me Elinor."

"I would like that, Elinor," Alden said. The way he said her name caused a fluttering in her stomach. An unwelcome fluttering. Why did this keep happening? She had no interest in Alden.

"Alden is not a common name, especially for the son of an earl," Elinor remarked. "May I ask where it is from?"

"It has ties to Old English and can be traced back to the given name Ealdwine, which translates to 'old friend'," Alden shared. "My mother heard it once and she thought it was a fitting name for me."

Elinor held his gaze as she admitted, "I think it fits you."

"You do?" he asked. "Because when I was younger, I would have given anything to have a common name like Matthew, Alexander or John. It would have stopped the teasing I was forced to endure at Eton."

"Not everyone is meant to fit in. Sometimes it is far better to stand out," Elinor said.

Alden cocked his head. "Do you wish to stand out?"

Elinor winced. "I did, at one point," she said. "But I attracted the attention of the Duke of Mardale."

"Is that the person you were supposed to marry?" Alden asked gently.

She nodded. "It was."

He leaned closer and said, "I can see why you ran away, especially since his person gives off an offensive odor." He paused. "That, and he is fifty years your senior."

"Thank you," she said, relief in her voice.

"For what?" Alden asked, his expression puzzled.

Elinor smiled. "For understanding," she said. "Many people thought I was foolish to run away from a marriage to a duke."

Alden returned her smile. "I am not one of them. In fact, it only confirms to me that you are indeed brave."

Before she could respond, Bryon stepped into the entry hall and announced, "Dinner is ready."

Alden glanced at the stairs. "Should we wait for your aunt?"

"I don't rightly know," Elinor replied. "She went to retrieve her bagpipes for the purpose of serenading us."

"Now you have me intrigued," he said, offering his arm. "I think it would be best if we waited for your aunt in the drawing room."

As Elinor accepted his arm, she felt a sudden jolt of awareness. She realized she had made a crucial error. She had developed feelings for Alden- feelings that she knew she had to push aside because they would do her no good.

Chapter Eight

As Alden escorted Elinor to the drawing room, he sensed a subtle but significant shift between them. He still held out hope that he could convince Elinor to become his wife. They got along well enough, and, truth be told, he found her rather intriguing. The only problem was that she was against a marriage of convenience. She wanted love, and that was something he could not offer. To him, marriage was a simple business transaction, nothing more.

When they reached the doorway of the drawing room, Alden noticed a piece of mistletoe hanging above them. Elinor followed his gaze, and he saw her visibly tense.

Turning her to face him, Alden said, "We are under the mistletoe. You know what that means."

"It means nothing," Elinor replied firmly.

"No, it means we have to kiss."

Elinor huffed. "We don't have to do anything."

Alden grinned, feeling the urge to tease her. "Careful, it almost seems like you don't want to kiss me."

"I can assure you that I do not."

"I think you do."

Tilting her chin up defiantly, Elinor responded, "You would be mistaken."

He leaned closer, their faces just inches apart. "Is the thought of kissing me so repulsive to you?" he asked softly.

"No, that is not it."

"Then what is it?" he asked, his voice a low murmur as he edged even closer.

Elinor's breath hitched, and her eyes dropped to his lips. "Must you stand so close?" she asked, her voice trembling slightly.

"Typically, people are close to one another when they kiss," he replied in a hoarse voice. He wanted to kiss her, feel her lips on his, but he didn't want to make her uncomfortable.

With great effort, he kissed her cheek and stepped back.

Elinor remained rooted in her spot, a blush spreading across her cheeks. "Thank you," she said. Perhaps his simple kiss on her cheek had more of an effect on her than he thought it would.

"For what?" he asked.

She brought her hand up to her cheek, where his lips had just been. "For respecting me enough to listen to what I want," she said.

"I will always listen to you," he assured her. "But I do think there will come a time when you want to kiss me. Badly."

"I do not think so."

"No, it is true," Alden said. "And when that happens, I will gladly oblige you."

Elinor dropped her hand to her side. "You are being rather cocky, sir."

"Am I?" he asked. "I merely speak the truth."

"I will never kiss you."

"Never say never," Alden said with a smirk.

Elinor rolled her eyes. "You are impossible," she said, her voice light, teasing.

Alden's smirk grew. "Yet, you still haven't moved from your spot under the mistletoe, making me wonder why that is."

"I am just merely waiting for my aunt to join us for dinner," Elinor said. "You could always move."

"Why would I?" he asked. "I want to kiss you."

Elinor stared back at him with disbelief. "Do you?"

"How can you even ask that question?" he inquired. "Why wouldn't I want to kiss a beautiful young woman?"

She bit her lower lip. "I'm afraid I have only been kissed once and it did not go well. The duke's breath smelled like garlic and his lips were hard."

Alden's smirk disappeared, replaced by a look of genuine concern. "I can see why you didn't find that pleasant. However, kissing can be quite enjoyable."

"I don't see how," she admitted.

Taking a step closer to Elinor, Alden gently ran his hand along her cheek. "Kissing is a way of expressing what you are truly feeling without using words."

Elinor held his gaze, her blue eyes filled with vulnerability. "My mother did say that kissing my father was one of her favorite things to do."

He chuckled. "That typically happens when you find the right person to kiss."

"But what if you kiss me and I don't like it?"

Alden moved closer, his movements slow and deliberate, waiting for any sign of discomfort from Elinor. "I promise that this time will be different. In fact, once you kiss me, you might never want to let me go. I am that good of a kisser."

"I suppose one kiss won't hurt," Elinor whispered as she closed her eyes.

Just as their lips were about to touch, a high-pitched sound caused him to jump back. He turned his head to see Mrs. Hardy standing next to them with a set of bagpipes in her hands.

"I hope I am not intruding," Mrs. Hardy said with a pointed look, clearly aware of what she had interrupted.

Elinor's hands flew up to her reddening cheeks. "We were standing under the mistletoe—"

"I know what you were doing," Mrs. Hardy interrupted. "But perhaps we can adjourn to the dining room so I can serenade you with my playing."

"Very well," Elinor said as she went to stand by her aunt.

Alden followed closely behind them, wondering what in the blazes had just happened. He had almost kissed Elinor, and he found that he wanted to. Desperately. He had never wanted to kiss someone as much as he wanted to kiss her. There was something about Elinor that drew him in, and he wasn't sure if he ever wanted to be let go.

Botheration.

This would not do. He just needed to convince her to marry him, not fall for her.

They arrived in the dining room, and he moved to pull out the chair for Elinor. She offered him a private smile and he was utterly charmed.

While he claimed his seat, Mrs. Hardy stood at the head of the table with the bagpipes, ready to play. "Now, please keep in mind that I am just a beginner."

"I am sure it will be delightful," Alden attempted.

Elinor met his gaze and shook her head.

Alden resisted the urge to smile before turning his attention back to Mrs. Hardy. She opened her mouth and proceeded to play. Loudly. And poorly. The shrill sound hurt his ears, but he tried to pretend that the noise didn't bother him.

After what felt like an eternity, but was probably just mere moments, Mrs. Hardy stopped playing and smiled. "What do you think?"

Terrible.

Awful.

But rather than insult her, he smiled and replied, "It was beautiful."

Mrs. Hardy gave him a smug smile. "I have been told that I can pick up instruments rather easily."

"That is evident by how well you play," Alden said, attempting to sound sincere.

Elinor giggled and brought her hand up to her lips. "I'm sorry, but it sounded like you were trying to slaughter a cat."

"Was it that bad?" Mrs. Hardy asked, her brow furrowing.

Alden cleared his throat. "Yes, but with the right teacher, you might be playing well in one or two… years."

Mrs. Hardy removed the bagpipes from around her and handed them to a footman. "Well, that only gives me the motivation to keep trying," she said as she went to sit down.

Elinor lowered her hand, her expression more serious. "I'm sorry. I hope I did not offend you."

"You could do no such thing, my dear," Mrs. Hardy said with a wave of her hand. "Besides, I know I need to practice more."

Footmen stepped forward and placed bowls of soup in front of them. Alden glanced down, fearing the worst, but to his pleasant surprise, it was pea soup.

Elinor must have seen his reaction because she said, "I thought you might be tired of Scottish food."

Alden reached for his spoon and dipped it in the soup. He brought it to his lips and savored the familiar taste. "It is delicious," he acknowledged.

"Mrs. Beaton can cook a wide array of foods. All you have to do is ask," Elinor informed him.

"Thank you," Alden said.

Elinor held his gaze for a long moment before she turned her attention towards her soup, and he couldn't help but notice the faint blush that colored her cheeks.

Turning towards him, Mrs. Hardy drew his attention by asking, "How did it go calling upon Mrs. MacBain?"

"It went well, I suppose," Alden responded.

Mrs. Hardy beamed, as if she were privy to a secret. "Isn't Mrs. MacBain a delight?"

"She is something, all right," Alden muttered. He truly didn't want to delve further into the topic with Mrs. Hardy.

"Oh, dear," Mrs. Hardy said. "Well, you will greatly enjoy Miss Isobel Fraser's company. She is quite an accomplished singer."

Elinor spoke up. "Yes, she often performs for the village."

Alden placed his spoon next to his empty bowl. He hadn't realized how hungry he had been until that precise moment. He found that he was not terribly fond of Scottish food and preferred the comforts of British food.

With a glance at his bowl, Elinor asked, "Would you care for more?"

"No, thank you," Alden replied.

"I will inform Mrs. Beaton that you enjoyed the soup," Elinor said.

Alden reluctantly dropped his gaze with Elinor, wondering what was going on with him. He found that he enjoyed being in Elinor's company far too much. Which would not do. He would need to be mindful to guard his heart, a heart that was supposed to be impenetrable.

The morning sun streamed into Elinor's bedchamber, casting a warm glow over her room as she lay in bed. She had slept restlessly, her dreams dominated by thoughts of Alden. Every time she closed her eyes, she saw him, becoming a rather bothersome presence. If she had her way, he would pack his trunks and leave the horse farm once and for all.

But he wouldn't do that.

It appeared that he wanted this horse farm as much as she did.

Elinor's mind kept replaying the moment they almost kissed. His breath had been warm, pleasantly free of any garlic scent, and his lips had looked so inviting, almost intoxicating. She had wanted to kiss him, and would have, if her aunt hadn't interrupted them. This would not do!

She needed to stop thinking about Alden and focus on getting him to leave. It was the simplest solution, especially since he wanted to sell the horse farm. If that happened, she and her aunt would be kicked out of their home. She couldn't let that happen.

A knock came at the door before it was pushed open, revealing Sophia. "Good morning," she greeted. "How did you sleep?"

"I slept well," she lied, forcing a smile.

"Shall we dress you for the day?" Sophia asked, walking over to the wardrobe. She pulled out a pale pink gown. "I do believe this dress will do nicely. What do you think?"

Elinor shrugged. "I do not care what dress I wear."

"You might not, but perhaps Mr. Dandridge will," Sophia responded with mirth in her voice. "I heard he was rather attentive to you last night."

"He was no such thing."

Sophia came to sit down on the edge of the bed. "Didn't you two almost kiss under the mistletoe?"

Elinor pressed her lips together. "How did you hear about that?"

"The whole manor is talking about it," Sophia declared. "It is not every day that the mistress of the manor has a handsome suitor."

"Mr. Dandridge is not my suitor," Elinor insisted.

Sophia winked. "Yes, Miss."

With a slight groan, Elinor asked, "Why don't you believe me?"

"Because your actions and words are saying two different things," Sophia declared, rising. "What is wrong with having a harmless flirtation with Mr. Dandridge?"

Elinor moved to place her legs over the side of the bed. "Mr. Dandridge and I just got caught up in the moment."

Sophia winked again. "Yes, Miss."

"Will you stop winking at me?" Elinor asked, exasperated. "You must trust me that nothing is going on between Mr. Dandridge and me."

"All right," Sophia said. "I will drop it… for now."

Elinor rose and sighed with relief. "Thank you."

Sophia laid the dress onto the bed. "Is there something wrong with Mr. Dandridge?" she asked. "Does he have only one leg or does his breath smell?"

"Nothing is wrong with Mr. Dandridge," Elinor asserted.

"Then why do you insist that you don't have any interest in him?" Sophia inquired.

Elinor sat down in front of the dressing table and reached for a brush. "He wants to marry for convenience, and I will only marry for love."

"Could it not turn into love?" Sophia asked.

"What if it doesn't?"

Sophia walked over and held her hand out for the brush. "You are many things, but a fortune teller is not one of them. Who knows what your future holds for you?"

Elinor removed the cap off the top of her head and placed it onto the dressing table. "Regardless, Mr. Dandridge wants to sell the horse farm. I can't allow that to happen. Lady Edith would be furious to know of his intentions."

"Can't you convince him otherwise?"

"How?" Elinor asked.

Sophia placed a hand on her hip and said, "Waggle your child-bearing hips around until he can think of little else."

"That is utterly ridiculous."

"Is it?" Sophia asked. "Mr. Dandridge already seems rather taken by you."

The door opened and Aunt Cecilia stepped into the room. "Mr. Dandridge has arrived for breakfast. I told him you would be down shortly."

Sophia made quick work as she placed Elinor's hair up into an elegant chignon. "Now on to your gown."

Once Elinor was dressed, she departed from her bedchamber and walked with her aunt down the hall.

Her aunt glanced her way. "Are you truly going to introduce him to Miss Fraser?" she inquired, her brow furrowed.

"There is nothing wrong with Miss Fraser," Elinor defended. "Besides, she is of marriageable age and is seeking a suitor. That is precisely what Mr. Dandridge is looking for."

"True," her aunt conceded, "but if you keep being so obvious about your intentions, he might catch on."

Elinor came to a stop and turned to face her aunt. "It is hardly obvious."

Her aunt gave her a knowing look. "Mrs. MacBain is desperate and would marry a scarecrow, assuming it came with money."

"Isobel is not desperate."

"Yet," her aunt pointed out. "The son of an earl is sniffing around this village and any one of these girls might gladly marry him."

Elinor frowned, crossing her arms. "Mr. Dandridge is not sniffing around."

Her aunt leaned forward and patted her cheek. "Of course not," she replied. "That is because you are enamored with him."

She rolled her eyes. "Not this again," she muttered as she continued down the hall.

As she descended the stairs, she saw Mr. Dandridge was standing in the entry hall, his hands clasped behind his back, looking deucedly handsome.

"Good morning," Alden greeted.

Elinor came to a stop in front of him, a smile playing on her lips. "Good morning," she said. "I do hope your cottage is still to your liking."

Alden nodded. "Yes, I have not encountered a single massive spider since I arrived."

"Just wait," Elinor teased.

"I would prefer not to," Alden responded. "Besides, your servants do a commendable job of scouring the cottage looking for any spiders."

Elinor felt her smile grow. "That is good to hear. I want you to be comfortable at the cottage."

Alden offered his arm. "Shall we adjourn to the dining room?"

With a glance over her shoulder, she said, "My aunt was right behind me, but I do not see her now."

"Perhaps she will meet us in the dining room," he suggested.

As he led her towards the dining room, Elinor asked, "Are you looking forward to meeting Miss Fraser today?"

"I am," Alden replied. "And who knows, she might be the next Mrs. Dandridge."

"Yes, wouldn't that be wonderful," Elinor muttered. The thought of Alden marrying anyone seemed to bother her. But she couldn't say as to why that was. She had no designs on him.

Alden eyed her curiously. "Unless you are interested in the position?"

Elinor huffed. "I already told you—"

"I know, but I am not going to stop asking," Alden said, interrupting her. "I think we would be good together. Don't you?"

"Marriage is so much more than being good together," Elinor remarked. "What of love?"

Alden's expression shifted, humor replaced by something

more solemn. "What of it?" he asked. "You speak of it as if it is the glue to hold a relationship together. But I believe it is more of mutual toleration."

"Mutual toleration? That is romantic," Elinor mocked.

Alden stopped and gently turned her to face him. "For a brief time, my parents fancied themselves in love, yet it led them to nothing but resentment. They prefer the company of others now."

"Not all marriages are like that," Elinor contended.

His eyes grew guarded. "Why?" he scoffed. "Because of your parents' example? They died too young. If they had lived longer, they would have grown to despise one another."

Elinor's eyes grew wide, disbelief washing over her. How could Alden say something so cruel to her? "That is awful of you to say," she admonished.

"It is the truth," he replied, his tone unwavering.

"No, it is *your* truth, and you are wrong about my parents," Elinor stated. "They loved each other until their last breaths."

Alden ran a hand through his hair, his frustration evident. "You are so naive in the ways of the world. Why would I expect you to understand?"

Elinor took a step closer to him, her chin tilted. "I'm sorry that your parents were terrible examples, but that doesn't give you the right to try to malign my parents' memory," she said. "And as for being naive, I freely admit that I am. I have lived a life that most people would dream of."

"Well, I hope that you can join us in the real world some-day," Alden stated with a slight bow.

"You are a muttonhead," Elinor said.

He grinned. "A muttonhead?" he asked. "Does your aunt know that you use such foul language?"

"In this case, I think she would encourage me to do so," Elinor responded.

"Elinor..." he sighed, his grin fading. "I don't want to

fight with you. We will just have to agree to disagree on this subject."

She took a step back. "I think that is fair, but I still won't marry you."

"You do realize that I am a son of an earl."

"Is that supposed to impress me?" she challenged.

"No, but it should persuade you, at least a little," Alden responded with a smug smile. "And imagine our children. They would be so attractive that they would outshine all other infants."

Elinor laughed. "Aren't all babies a blessing?"

"Are they?" Alden asked. "I would think no one would willingly want an ugly baby."

"Now you are just spouting nonsense," Elinor said. "Let us enjoy breakfast before we must leave to call on Miss Fraser."

Chapter Nine

Alden sat in the coach across from Elinor and her lady's maid. The rhythmic clatter of wheels on the cobblestone road accompanied them as they made their way to call upon Miss Fraser.

He fervently hoped that this visit would go more smoothly than his previous encounter with Mrs. MacBain. He shuddered at the thought of all her children. He wasn't ready to be a father. Not that he was opposed to children. He simply wanted to raise them differently than he had been.

His parents had always treated him with a certain cold indifference, never expecting much from him. No matter his accomplishments, he doubted he would ever earn their approval. But that didn't stop him from trying. He had a plan to become one of the largest landowners in England, hoping that such an achievement would finally make them proud.

The coach hit a rut in the road, causing it to jolt to the side. Elinor reached out to steady herself, her gloved fingers gripping the edge of the seat. He took a moment to briefly admire her. Her dark hair was piled elegantly atop her head, with two long tendrils framing her face. Not only was she beautiful, but that beauty touched the depths of her soul, reaching every inch of her heart and how she perceived the world.

Elinor was an anomaly to him. She was fiercely independent, yet she spoke of love as if it were a tangible, attainable thing.

"Is everything all right?" Elinor asked, breaking through his thoughts.

Realizing that he had been caught staring, Alden smiled. "I do apologize, but I was woolgathering."

"A terrible habit to have," Elinor teased, her eyes sparkling with amusement.

He glanced at the window, feeling the need to steer the conversation. "Will you tell me more about Miss Fraser?"

Elinor adjusted the blanket around her waist. "Gladly," she replied. "Isobel is a pleasant young woman who was raised to be a lady. Her father is Laird Ewan Fraser of Glenfinnan and she holds herself with the epitome of grace."

"May I ask why she isn't married?" Alden asked.

She gave him an exasperated look. "That is rather an insensitive question. There could be a myriad of reasons why she is not married, but I am not privy to any of them."

"Is something wrong with her?" Alden pressed, unable to help himself.

"Just because a woman is not married, that does not mean something is wrong with her," Elinor said, her tone sharp. "Do you think something is wrong with me?"

Alden shook his head. "No, but you are not married by choice."

"Yes, and I believe I have sufficiently explained my reasonings."

"You have, but—" Alden began.

Elinor cut him off. "Why do you insist on doing that? Anything you say before the 'but' is hogwash."

He sighed, frustration seeping into his voice. "You are rather infuriating."

"Thank you," Elinor said with a smile.

"That wasn't a compliment."

"Perhaps not, but I took it as one, seeing as it was coming from you," Elinor remarked.

Turning his attention towards the lady's maid, Alden asked, "Is Miss Sidney always like this?"

"Worse, sir," Sophia said with a grin.

Elinor lifted an eyebrow as she turned towards her lady's maid. "Whose side are you on?" she asked, her voice holding mirth.

Sophia laughed. "Yours, and always yours, Miss Sidney," she responded. "However, we both know that you like to debate."

"Debate?" Alden interjected. "That is a nice word for saying 'argue'."

"There is nothing wrong with a lively debate," Elinor defended.

Alden gave her a knowing look. "You aren't looking for a debate. You just want everyone to agree with you."

"And you don't do the same thing?" Elinor retorted.

"Touché," Alden said.

He turned his head towards the window and noticed the long, tree-lined drive as they approached the estate. As the coach rolled to a stop, he took in the sight of the imposing structure before them. The manor house was a stately edifice, its stone façade softened by a tapestry of ivy that climbed the walls.

The coach dipped to the side as the footman stepped off his perch. The door was opened, and Alden stepped out. He turned back to help the ladies out of the coach.

He offered his arm to Elinor, and they started walking towards the manor. The door promptly opened, and the butler greeted them. "Good morning, Miss Sidney," he said, standing to the side. "Lady Glenfinnan and her daughter, Miss Fraser, are expecting you."

The butler led them into the drawing room and announced them.

A tall, red-headed older woman smiled warmly at them. "Miss Sidney. Mr. Dandridge," she said. "Welcome to our manor."

Alden bowed. "Thank you, my lady." As he straightened up, his gaze shifted to the young red-headed woman beside her. He noticed her eyes were downcast, and her hands were clasped nervously in front of her.

Lady Glenfinnan gently nudged her daughter with her shoulder, encouraging her to speak. "Do you wish to say anything, Isobel?" she prompted.

Miss Fraser shook her head.

An exasperated look came to Lady Glenfinnan's face. "Do make an effort, Dear," she said, her voice strained.

Bringing her head up, Miss Fraser briefly met Alden's gaze. "It is a pleasure to meet you, sir." Her words lacked any real emotion.

"Don't forget to curtsy," Lady Glenfinnan muttered under her breath.

Miss Fraser dropped into an exaggerated curtsy, looking entirely out of place in the drawing room.

Lady Glenfinnan looked heavenward. "Give me strength with this one," she whispered before gesturing towards the settee. "Would either of you care for a cup of tea?"

Elinor spoke up. "I would greatly appreciate one," she said as she approached the settee. "It is rather cold outside."

"That it is," Lady Glenfinnan agreed.

Miss Fraser sat down on the settee and reached for a book. She opened it and settled back into her seat.

Alden went to sit down next to Elinor and pointed towards the book in Miss Fraser's hand. "May I ask what you are reading?"

Miss Fraser's eyes flashed with annoyance before lowering the book. "*Principia*," she responded.

"Ah, you are interested in physics, then?" Alden asked.

She nodded. "I am," she confirmed. "This is the book where Isaac Newton introduced his three laws of motion and so much more."

Lady Glenfinnan interjected, "Dear, put the book down. We have guests."

With great reluctance, Miss Fraser closed the book and placed it onto her lap. "Are you familiar with the law of universal gravitation?" she asked, addressing Alden.

Alden put his hand up. "I'm afraid not. I attended some lectures about the subject at Oxford, but I studied Latin."

"Latin?" Miss Fraser repeated. "What a useless thing to study."

"Isobel…" Lady Glenfinnan warned.

Miss Fraser continued. "I am just merely saying that if I had been lucky enough to be born a man, I would not have wasted my time at university on Latin."

"What is wrong with Latin?" Alden asked.

"It is boring," Miss Fraser responded. "I would prefer to read books by Galileo Galilei or Daniel Bernoulli. I find fluid dynamics to be rather fascinating, especially Bernoulli's principle."

Alden quickly realized that he had little in common with Miss Fraser, considering he was at a loss for words. He knew little about physics. "I am not familiar with that principle," he admitted.

Lady Glenfinnan cleared her throat, drawing her daughter's attention. "Will you pour tea for our guests and stop with this physics nonsense?"

"It isn't nonsense," Miss Fraser defended. "But, yes, I will pour. After all, what else am I good for?"

Turning her attention towards Alden, Lady Glenfinnan brought a smile to her face. "I do apologize for Isobel. She can be rather passionate about physics."

Alden put his hand up. "You do not need to apologize. I appreciate a young woman who finds her passion."

Miss Fraser extended him a teacup. "Thank you for saying so. May I ask what your passion is?"

"My passion?" Alden asked.

"Yes, I am passionate about physics, my mother is passionate about marrying me off, and Elinor is passionate about the horse farm," Miss Fraser said.

Alden accepted the teacup as he debated about his answer. What was he passionate about? After a long moment, he replied, "I suppose my passion is to become one of the largest landowners in England."

Miss Fraser looked unimpressed by what he had revealed. "Do you at least like to read?"

"I do," Alden responded.

"What was the last book you read?" Miss Fraser pressed.

Alden shifted uncomfortably in his seat. "It has been a while since I have had the time to read a book."

Miss Fraser frowned as she handed out the rest of the teacups and saucers, clearly unimpressed by his admission. "It is a shame that you don't take advantage of the written word, sir."

"That is enough, Isobel," Lady Glenfinnan insisted. "You are not being a very good hostess to our guests."

"I do not take offense, my lady. I find Miss Fraser's frankness to be refreshing," Alden said.

"You do?" Lady Glenfinnan asked.

Alden grinned. "I do," he replied, hoping to earn Miss Fraser's approval. "I do believe a woman's greatest weapon is her mind."

Rather than look pleased by his remark, Miss Fraser opened her book in her lap and started reading once more.

Miss Fraser was pretty enough to tempt him with her red hair and striking blue eyes, but it was obvious that she found him lacking.

Alden glanced at Elinor and noticed a smile playing on her lips. It almost appeared as if she were enjoying herself.

Elinor caught his eyes and her smile grew. "Isobel isn't wrong. You should be reading more books."

"I read plenty," Alden defended.

"Yet, you can't name the last book you read?" Elinor challenged.

Alden leaned closer to her and asked, "Whose side are you on?"

Elinor patted his sleeve. "I am just a neutral observer to all of this."

"Traitor," Alden muttered playfully.

Lady Glenfinnan held her hand out to her daughter. "Give me the book," she ordered.

With a slight huff, Miss Fraser closed the book and placed it in her mother's hand.

"Now, where were we?" Lady Glenfinnan asked, placing the book onto a table.

———————⌒————————

Elinor was trying hard not to laugh, but this was going precisely how she expected it to go. Miss Fraser was many things, but she cared more about physics than anything. It had always been this way. Many people in the village considered her odd, but Elinor didn't. She found her to be a delight and rather enjoyed conversing with her.

Miss Fraser leaned forward in her seat and retrieved her cup of tea. She met Alden's gaze and said, "I understand you are looking for a wife."

Alden had just brought the cup to his lips and choked slightly as he took a sip. "I am," he confirmed.

"I will do it," Miss Fraser began, "assuming you are serious about it being a marriage of convenience. I can focus on my studies in physics, and you can focus on whatever it is that interests you."

"Perhaps we should start by you telling me about yourself," Alden said.

Miss Fraser took a sip of her tea before lowering it to her lap. "I am eight and ten years old. My parents said I don't have to have a Season if I get married to you," she shared. "I was worried that you would be unfortunate-looking but you are tolerable."

"Tolerable?" Alden repeated.

"I am partial to Scottish men with red hair, but I suppose a dark-haired Englishman will do," Miss Fraser responded.

Alden frowned. "How generous of you," he muttered.

Lady Glenfinnan spoke up. "Isobel is just teasing you," she rushed out. "She has no qualms with Englishmen, considering she went to boarding school in Northumberland. We ensured she was properly educated."

"I do hope you don't take issue with me dressing up in men's clothing to attend lectures on physics," Miss Fraser said.

"That is quite scandalous," Alden stated.

"Only if you get caught, and I have no intention of doing so," Miss Fraser said. "Now, shall we talk about marital duties?"

Alden's brow shot up. "I beg your pardon?"

"I suppose you will require an heir, but I am willing to give you one child. I can't predict if it is male or female, though," Miss Fraser responded, her face expressionless. "Do we have a deal?"

Elinor brought her hand up to her lips as she tried to hide her smile. It would not do well if it looked like she was enjoying this exchange.

Alden stared at Miss Fraser like she had sprouted two heads. "I... uh... don't know what to say," he stuttered out.

Miss Fraser looked unconcerned. "Also, more importantly, I do not like horses. I was tossed off a horse when I was younger and I was unconscious for a day. Ever since then, I have avoided those dreadful animals."

"Perhaps we should give Mr. Dandridge some time to think on this, Dear," Lady Glenfinnan said. "I do think your frankness has caught him by surprise."

"I think it is better if we are honest with each other, so we know what to expect from one another," Miss Fraser said.

Alden leaned forward and placed his cup and saucer on the table, looking visibly relieved by what Miss Fraser had shared. "I appreciate your honesty, but my great-aunt did specify that I must find someone that is particular to horses," he shared. "So I am afraid we would not suit."

"Very well. If that is your decision, I shall respect it," Miss Fraser said, turning towards her mother. "I'm tired. May I be excused now?"

Lady Glenfinnan gave her daughter an exasperated look. "Not until our guests leave," she replied.

Elinor glanced over at Alden and saw his jaw was clenched. He did not appear to be amused by Miss Fraser's antics like she was. Perhaps it would be best if they left.

"We should be going," Elinor said, placing her cup and saucer onto the tray. "I have work that I must see to."

"Must you go so soon?" Lady Glenfinnan asked.

Rising, Elinor nodded. "I shall return to call upon Isobel in a few days, assuming that is agreeable."

Isobel perked up. "Yes, I would greatly enjoy that."

Alden had risen and bowed. "Ladies, it was a pleasure to meet both of you," he said politely before offering his arm to Elinor. "Shall we?"

Elinor accepted his arm. "Thank you, Mr. Dandridge."

As they walked towards the main door, Lady Glenfinnan followed them to the door and said in a hushed voice, "Isobel can be rather brazen, but she really does have a tender heart. I wanted you to know that."

"I have no doubt," Alden said with a tip of his head.

Elinor dropped into a curtsy. "My lady," she murmured.

After they stepped outside, Alden dropped his arm and turned towards her. "No," he simply said.

"No?"

Alden pointed towards the manor. "How could you think I would be interested in someone like Miss Fraser?"

"If you recall, your requirement was only that she was beautiful," Elinor defended. "Is Miss Fraser not to your liking?"

He ran a hand through his hair. "She is pretty, but she only finds me tolerable."

"I would not take offense to that," Elinor said.

"I don't, but I…" His words trailed off. "She spoke of marital relations."

Elinor giggled, bringing her hand up to cover her mouth. "That might have been my favorite part of the whole conversation."

Alden pointed at her. "I'm beginning to think that you are the problem."

"Me?" Elinor asked.

"First, you introduced me to Mrs. MacBain, who has twenty children…."

Elinor spoke over him. "She has six children."

"… then you introduce me to someone that is clearly more interested in physics than being a wife," Alden said.

"You are upset," Elinor remarked.

Alden tossed his hands up in the air. "Of course I am upset. How am I ever going to get married when the young women you are introducing me to are entirely unacceptable."

Elinor tilted her head. "Perhaps if you gave me more instruction other than requiring that they are beautiful and desire to get married at once."

"There must be one normal young woman in this whole village," Alden declared.

"You haven't met Maisie Cowen yet," Elinor attempted. "She is beautiful, well-read and gracious."

Alden took a step closer to her. "This whole problem could be solved if you agreed to marry me."

Elinor smirked. "Would I be required to have marital relations with you?" she quipped.

"This is not funny."

"It is, just a little bit," Elinor joked. "Perhaps we should finish this conversation in the coach, considering it is rather cold."

Alden held his hand out towards the coach. "After you," he said.

Once Elinor was situated in the coach, her lady's maid sat next to her, and Alden sat across from her.

The coach slowly moved forward and Alden gave her a stern look. "My great-aunt said that you would help me."

"And I am trying to," Elinor lied, feeling the familiar guilt that was growing with each passing day. "You will like Maisie Cowen. Trust me."

"What is wrong with her?" Alden demanded.

"There is nothing wrong with her," Elinor responded. "Just as there was nothing wrong with Mrs. MacBain and Miss Fraser."

Alden started tapping his foot, frustration evident on his brow. "I do not have time for games. I need a wife, and quickly."

Elinor smiled, hoping to disarm him. "And you will get one... in due time."

"I don't have time," he argued. "There must be one agreeable young woman in this entire god-forsaken village."

Her smile vanished. "You are being rather rude, and I won't stand for it. This village is made up of good, hard-working, honorable people."

Leaning forward, Alden asked, "Do you know what happens if I don't marry?"

"You won't inherit the horse farm," Elinor responded.

"Precisely, and I will have nothing," Alden said.

Elinor clasped her hands in front of her. "You won't have nothing," she attempted. "You are still the second son of an earl."

"Who only has a small inheritance to his name," Alden stated.

"That is more than some people have."

Alden's eyes flickered with determination. "I need to inherit this horse farm so I can sell it and use the money to buy land in England."

"Why not keep it?" Elinor asked. "That is what your Great-aunt Edith would want."

"What do you know of my great-aunt's intentions?" Alden demanded.

Elinor held his gaze. "Apparently, more than you do," she said. "This was her grandfather's horse farm and he built it up to what it is today. It means something to her."

Alden sat back in his seat. "Well, it means nothing to me."

"That is a shame," Elinor said. "For it is more than a horse farm, it is my place of refuge. I wish you could see it the same way."

"I don't need a refuge," Alden responded.

"Doesn't everyone need a refuge, at least for a little while?" Elinor asked.

Alden looked heavenward. "No, I need a wife, not a useless horse farm."

Turning her head towards the window, Elinor knew there was no point in continuing this argument with Alden. He wasn't being reasonable. He just saw the horse farm as a means to an end, and not for what it truly was worth. She couldn't let him get married and sell it. She was responsible for the horse farm, and she took that role very seriously.

Chapter Ten

Alden's eyes flew open as he lay in bed, the peace of early morning shattered by an obnoxious, blaring sound. He groaned, throwing off his blankets and walking over to the window to see what had disturbed his slumber.

Pulling aside the heavy drapes, he peered outside and saw Mrs. Hardy standing a short distance away, playing the bagpipes. Good gads! What was she thinking playing the bagpipes at such an early hour and so close to his cottage?

A brisk knock came at the door before it was opened, revealing his valet. "I see that you are awake," Hastings said, stepping inside.

"How could I not be with that infernal racket?" Alden asked as he turned to face his valet. "I suppose I should get ready for the day."

Hastings walked over to the wardrobe and retrieved his clothing. As he laid the clothing onto the bed, he asked, "Dare I ask if you have convinced Miss Sidney to marry you?"

"No, not yet," Alden admitted, running a hand through his disheveled hair. "She is adamant that she will only marry for love."

"And you can't give her that?"

Alden looked at Hastings like he was a simpleton. "Of course not! Everyone knows that there is no place for love in a marriage."

"I love my wife," Hastings said simply.

"But for how long?" Alden questioned. "Eventually, you will tire of her."

Hastings grinned. "Considering I have been married for ten years now, I think it is going well for us."

Alden walked over to the bed and began dressing. "I'm sorry, but I'm afraid I cannot risk it."

"May I speak freely, sir?" Hastings asked, his tone respectful yet insistent.

Pulling his shirt over his head, Alden said, "I would prefer it."

"I think you should open your heart to Miss Sidney and see what happens," Hastings remarked.

"Why would I do that?"

"Because you smile every time you say her name," Hastings pointed out.

Alden reached for the cravat, finding his valet's observations utterly ridiculous. He didn't smile when he said Elinor's name. Did he? "Regardless, that doesn't mean I love her."

"I never said you did, but I think she means more to you than you are letting on," Hastings said.

"But she wants nothing to do with me," Alden remarked as he walked over to the mirror to adjust his cravat.

"Then change her mind."

Alden's hands paused as he met Hastings' gaze in the mirror. "And how, pray tell, do I do that?"

Hastings smiled. "Convince her that you are worth taking a chance on," he said.

"Don't you think I have been trying to do just that?"

Reaching for the jacket on the bed, Hastings walked it over to Alden. "I think you should try to make her jealous."

Alden accepted the jacket. "And how do I go about doing that?"

"You should take a sudden interest in one of the young women that Miss Sidney introduced you to," Hastings responded.

"That is quite impossible, considering I would not suit with Mrs. MacBain or Miss Fraser," Alden said.

Hastings shrugged, a twinkle of mischief in his eyes. "Sometimes the impossible is what makes the game interesting," he said. "What about Miss Cowen? Is Miss Sidney not introducing you to her today?"

"Yes, but I have no idea what she is like," Alden said.

"Does it matter?" Hastings inquired. "It is not as if you have to marry the young woman."

Alden slipped the jacket on. "And what if Miss Sidney doesn't care that I am showing interest in Miss Cowen?"

"She will," Hastings said confidently. "It has been my experience that people tend to want what they can't have."

"It just seems like a game that I don't want to play," Alden remarked.

Hastings picked up the discarded clothing from the floor. "Courting is a game, one that you intend to win," he said. "Besides, what do you have to lose?"

Alden winced as the bagpipe music seemed to grow louder, making it almost impossible to think. "I hate bagpipes," he muttered.

"I rather enjoy them, but Mrs. Hardy is awful," Hastings remarked.

"She just started playing."

Hastings glanced at the window. "Dying animals sound better than her playing the bagpipes."

Alden chuckled. "I agree, wholeheartedly." He walked over to the door. "I am going to ask her to stop."

"I wish you luck," Hastings said.

As Alden departed from his bedchamber, he headed down

the stairs and stepped out into the chilly morning air. He approached Mrs. Hardy from behind. He didn't wish to startle her, so he gently tapped her on the shoulder.

Mrs. Hardy stopped playing the bagpipes and let out a slight scream. She turned around and her eyes grew wide. "Mr. Dandridge, you frightened me."

"I'm sorry. That was not my intention," Alden said. "May I ask why you are playing the bagpipes at such an early hour?"

Mrs. Hardy smiled. "I thought you might enjoy waking up to the soothing sounds of the bagpipes."

Alden resisted the urge to laugh. There was nothing soothing about the bagpipes, especially when Mrs. Hardy played them. "That was kind of you," he said.

"Shall I keep playing?" Mrs. Hardy asked, bringing the reed to her lips.

"Good heavens, no!" Alden rushed out. "I mean… you have already played for so long. I don't want you to get tired."

Mrs. Hardy bobbed her head. "Perhaps I should stop for a little while and catch my breath."

"I think that is a wonderful idea," Alden said. "May I escort you back to the manor?"

"Yes, the coach is just around the bend," Mrs. Hardy replied.

As they started walking towards the coach, Alden asked, "Do you enjoy playing the bagpipes?"

"I do, and I think I am getting quite good at it," Mrs. Hardy replied.

Alden didn't dare contradict her, but he suspected she was getting worse with every blow into the reed. "Well, practice does make perfect."

Mrs. Hardy beamed. "I will be happy to wake you up tomorrow with the bagpipes."

"That is kind of you to offer, but I prefer to wake up gradually," Alden responded.

"I understand," Mrs. Hardy said. "Furthermore, tomorrow is Christmas."

Alden glanced over at her. "I had almost forgotten about Christmas."

Mrs. Hardy gave him an understanding look. "You must be sad to not be with your family for Christmas."

"Quite the contrary, I'm afraid. My family does not make a big ado out of Christmas," Alden admitted. "It is just another day."

"That is a shame," Mrs. Hardy responded. "I do want to thank you for convincing Elinor to decorate the manor for the holiday."

Alden brushed off her praise. "It was nothing."

"It was more than nothing," Mrs. Hardy remarked. "I have been trying since we moved here but Elinor had been insistent. She keeps up a strong façade, but I know she is hurting. Deeply. Christmas is hard on her."

"She has told me as much."

Mrs. Hardy tipped her head. "Elinor must trust you if she is willing to confide in you," she said.

"We are friends."

"I see," Mrs. Hardy said as she approached the coach. Alden held his hand out to assist her inside. Once she was situated, he climbed in and sat across from her. He reached for the blanket and placed it onto Mrs. Hardy's lap.

The coach began moving and Alden turned his attention towards the window. He watched the horses grazing in the distance.

Mrs. Hardy's voice broke the silence. "It is rather idyllic, is it not?"

"It is," Alden was forced to admit.

"I hope you don't mind but Elinor told me that you intend to sell the horse farm once you are married," Mrs. Hardy said. "I do believe that is a mistake."

Alden brought his gaze to meet hers. "Do you now?"

"I do, and that is because Elinor loves this horse farm," Mrs. Hardy replied. "It is a part of her."

"I respect that, but I must do what is the best for me," Alden said.

Mrs. Hardy considered him for a moment before saying, "That is the problem. You are only thinking about yourself."

"Who else would I think about?" Alden asked, a hint of defensiveness in his tone.

As she removed the bagpipes off her shoulders, Mrs. Hardy replied, "There comes a point in our lives when we must realize what is worth fighting for."

Alden lifted his brow. "And what should I fight for?"

"I can't tell you that," Mrs. Hardy replied. "Everyone must decide that for themselves."

"What do you fight for?" Alden asked, genuinely curious.

Mrs. Hardy smiled. "That is easy," she replied. "I fight for my niece, Elinor. We help one another, but I suspect she doesn't need me as much as I need her."

The coach came to a stop in front of the manor and a footman came around to open the door. After Mrs. Hardy stepped out, he followed her onto solid ground, feeling the cool morning air on his face.

"Now, if you'll excuse me, I need to go lie down since I woke up entirely too early to play for you," Mrs. Hardy said as they stepped into the entry hall. "You might be interested to know that Elinor is in her study."

"At this hour?"

Mrs. Hardy laughed. "She lives and breathes for this horse farm. You would be wise to remember that."

Alden didn't need to be told twice. He found he was rather eager to see Elinor this morning. Quite frankly, he was eager to see her all the time. She was giving him far too many reasons to smile, which was beginning to be problematic.

Elinor sat at the desk as she reviewed the accounts. The early morning light filtered through the window, casting a soft glow over the papers strewn across her desk. Tomorrow was Christmas, and though memories kept flooding her mind, she repeatedly pushed them away, determined to focus on her tasks.

Alden's voice broke through the silence. "Good morning," he greeted.

She looked up, surprised to see him leaning against the door frame, a soft smile playing on his lips. "What are you doing up so early?" she asked.

He pushed off from the door frame and walked closer to the desk. "I could ask you the same question."

"I'm afraid I couldn't sleep," she admitted. "There is always something to do."

"I wish that was my reason to be awake, but it is because your aunt was playing the bagpipes just outside of my window," Alden shared.

Elinor grinned. "That sounds like my aunt."

With a glance over his shoulder, Alden asked, "Which one of us is going to tell her that she is awful?"

"That is not a conversation I wish to have with her."

Alden sighed, taking a seat in the chair facing the desk. "Neither do I. When are we going to call upon Miss Cowen?"

"After breakfast, assuming that is all right with you," Elinor responded.

"It is," Alden said. He then studied her intently. "How are you faring?"

"I am well," she answered, her tone was less convincing than she hoped.

Alden's gaze didn't waver. "Are you?" he asked gently. "I

only ask because tomorrow is Christmas and I know that this time of year is hard for you."

Elinor felt her back grow rigid. "I will be fine."

"It is all right if you aren't," Alden said.

"I said I will be fine," she responded curtly. She didn't want to have this conversation with him... with anyone, for that matter.

Alden put his hand up. "I did not mean to upset you," he said. "But if you wish to talk, I am here to listen."

Elinor knew that Alden was only trying to help so she softened her tone. "That is kind of you, but I just try to keep myself busy around this time. The less I think of it, the better."

"I think that is a mistake," he said.

"Do you?" Elinor asked, her voice holding a warning. "And why, pray tell, is that?"

Alden continued. "I think it is best if you talk about your loved ones that have passed on. It helps you remember them."

Elinor scoffed. "You would know this how?"

His eyes grew sad. "I have lost loved ones over the years and each loss leaves an imprint on my soul."

"I'm sorry," Elinor responded.

"What was your mother like?" he asked.

She closed the ledger in front of her and abruptly rose. "I can't do this now," she said, her voice strained. "Shall we adjourn to the dining room?"

"We can, but I still would like to know," Alden insisted.

Elinor hesitated, then slowly returned to her seat. "My mother was my best friend. It didn't start off that way. When I was younger, I thought she was the fun killer, but I have since learned that it was her way of protecting me."

"Fun killer?" Alden asked, his lips twitching.

A smile played on Elinor's lips. "Yes, someone that kills all the fun. You must understand that I was rather adventurous when I was a child and spent most of my time in the woodlands."

Alden laughed. "That does not surprise me in the least."

"When I was younger, I started riding my horse without a saddle," Elinor admitted. "My mother was mortified and forbid me from doing so."

"You must have been quite the handful," Alden quipped.

Elinor nodded. "I was, considering I wore men's clothing and rode astride."

Alden's smile widened. "That does not surprise me at all."

A smile tugged at Elinor's lips as she remembered. "My mother just wanted to keep me safe, even when I was determined to be reckless," she said. "But what I miss the most about her is how she looked at me. Her eyes always told me that she loved me, even when her words did not."

Settling back in his seat, Alden asked, "And what of your father?"

Her smile grew even more. "My father was the reason I was so reckless. He convinced me that I could do anything if I put my mind to it. He was my greatest supporter, and I loved our rides together."

In a gentle voice, Alden asked, "How did they die?"

Her face fell. "Consumption."

"I'm sorry," Alden said.

"There is nothing worse than watching your parents waste away until they take their last breaths," Elinor said, her voice trembling as she fought back the tears. "My father was the first to go."

Alden leaned forward in his seat, his eyes filled with compassion. "I know it is not the same, but my grandmother died from consumption. I held her hand until the very end."

"Were you close to your grandmother?" Elinor asked.

"I was," Alden confirmed. "She didn't look at me like the spare. She loved me for who I was, and not my position at birth."

Elinor nodded in understanding. "My parents never made me feel less since I wasn't born a male."

"I'm glad," Alden said.

"Just so you know, I am glad that we are friends," Elinor responded. "I don't have very many of those, at least not anymore. Most of my friends abandoned me when I refused to marry the duke."

"That was wrong of them."

Elinor shook her head. "I don't blame them. I was a walking scandal and that is the last thing a woman in the *ton* wishes to be around."

"How is it that you escaped my notice when you debuted?" Alden asked.

She shrugged one shoulder. "I don't know, but I did not spend much time with rakes."

"I am not a rake," he defended.

"If you say so."

"I do."

Elinor laughed. "I believe you, but you were rather cocky when we first met, irritatingly so."

"And now?"

Rising, Elinor smoothed down her pale pink gown. "You are much more tolerable."

Alden rose with her. "Only tolerable?"

Elinor came around her desk and stood in front of him, a playful smile on her lips. "You still vex me."

"I have to keep things interesting between us," Alden responded as he offered his arm. "Shall we adjourn to the dining room now?"

She took his arm, and the smell of lavender drifted off her person. He resisted the urge to lean closer to her.

As they walked towards the dining room, Elinor asked, "Do you have any Christmas traditions that I should know about?"

"I'm afraid not," Alden responded. "I have spent more Christmases alone than with my family."

"That is awful."

"No, it is familiar," Alden said. "I don't know what I would do if my parents suddenly wished to spend time with me."

Elinor glanced over at him, her eyes softening with sympathy. "I'm sorry," she said, knowing her words were wholly inadequate.

"Do not feel bad for me. I have learned to make do," Alden remarked. "I prefer spending Christmas alone."

"Well, you aren't going to be alone tomorrow. We will spend the day together," Elinor insisted.

Alden tipped his head. "I have no objections."

"Good, because you have little choice in the matter," Elinor joked. "What should we do? We could start with a morning ride?"

"In this weather? I think not," Alden asked.

Elinor stepped into the dining room and dropped Alden's arm. "It is not that bad," she attempted as she went to sit down.

Alden claimed the seat next to her. "Although, going on a morning ride does sound more enjoyable than listening to your aunt playing the bagpipes."

"You make a good point," Elinor said, reaching for a cup of chocolate. "And I will be sure to protect you from any spiders we see."

"How are you not afraid of spiders?"

Elinor took a sip and returned the cup to her saucer. "Oh, I am terrified of them. I just had to tease you about them."

Alden chuckled. "So you recognize how immensely large house spiders are?"

"They are ginormous," Elinor declared. "I once woke up to one that was in the corner of my canopy bed. I think I woke the whole household with my screams."

He tsked. "Yet you made me believe I was the only one who was afraid of them."

"I had to humble you one way or another."

Shifting in his seat, Alden asked, "Why did you need to humble me?"

"You were just like every gentleman in high Society when you first arrived," Elinor responded. "Cocky. Inconsiderate. Thinking you were god's gift to women."

"And now?"

Elinor met his gaze. "I told you- you are tolerable now."

He huffed. "I am more than tolerable."

"What are you then?"

Alden considered her for a moment before saying, "I am chivalrous, and I have refined manners."

"Says the man that is afraid of spiders and was screaming about them like a lunatic," Elinor retorted.

"It is hardly my fault. I could have put a saddle on that spider and ridden it," Alden said.

Elinor laughed loudly. "That is absurd."

"Perhaps, but I prefer the small spiders in England."

A footman placed a plate of food down in front of them and Elinor reached for her fork and knife.

Alden took a sip of his drink before placing it back down onto the table. "This is nice," he admitted. "I haven't enjoyed myself like this in a long time."

"Nor I," Elinor agreed.

He held her gaze for a moment before saying, "I am glad that we are friends, Elinor."

Friends.

Yes, that is what she wanted to be.

So why was her heart pounding in her chest?

Elinor lowered her gaze to her plate, not understanding the churning of emotions within her. No good would come from allowing her feelings to deepen for Alden. Yet her treacherous heart did not seem to listen- or care.

Chapter Eleven

Alden stared out the window of the coach as it rumbled towards Miss Cowen's manor, his thoughts churning with a mixture of anticipation and doubt. He didn't have high hopes when meeting this young woman, but he hoped he could at least convince Elinor that he was interested. Perhaps, if he made her jealous, she might come to her senses and marry him. He hoped so, considering he rather enjoyed spending time with Elinor and wouldn't mind continuing to do so in the future.

Elinor's voice broke through the silence. "We are almost there."

Alden turned his gaze back to her, studying her calm demeanor. "Are you sure that I will like this Miss Cowen?"

She nodded. "Yes, Maisie is a dear friend. She wants nothing more than to be a wife and a mother."

"Does she take issue that it will be a marriage of convenience?"

"She has no objections," Elinor assured him.

Alden eyed Elinor curiously, his skepticism evident. "And you are quite certain that nothing is wrong with her?"

Elinor looked amused. "I am, just as I have assured you before."

"Does she have an impairment of some kind or hordes of children tucked away in the cupboards?" Alden pressed, a hint of humor in his voice.

With a laugh, Elinor responded, "She is nine and ten years old and has no children or impairments that I know of."

"You mentioned she is well-read, but will she be sneaking into lectures on physics?" Alden inquired.

"I promise you that Maisie has no intentions of doing something so scandalous. She is a lady and prefers the comforts of home," Elinor replied with a knowing smile.

The coach came to a stop in front of a modest-sized manor and Alden stepped out. Once he was on solid ground, he reached back to assist Elinor and her lady's maid out. He tucked Elinor's hand into the crook of his arm and led her towards the main door.

Alden knocked on the door and took a step back, his eyes scanning the well-maintained surroundings.

The door was promptly opened by a white-haired woman. "Good morning," she greeted warmly. "Please come in."

Alden stepped into the small entry hall with Elinor still on his arm. "Is Miss Cowen available for callers?" he asked.

The white-haired woman smiled broadly. "She is," she confirmed. "Please, follow me."

As they stepped into the drawing room, Alden's eyes immediately fell on a young woman sprawled out on the settee, a pillow over her face. "Is that you, Mrs. Campbell?" she asked, her voice muffled.

"Yes, and guests have arrived," Mrs. Campbell replied.

Miss Cowen moved the pillow off her face and quickly sat up. She was an attractive woman with an oval face, pale skin and blonde hair that was tied into a bun at the base of her neck. "Good morning," she said in an overly cheerful voice. "What a lovely day we are having. Please come sit."

Elinor gestured towards Alden and provided the introductions. "Miss Maisie Cowen, please allow me to introduce you to Mr. Dandridge, the great-nephew of Lady Edith."

Alden bowed. "It is a pleasure to meet you, Miss Cowen."

Miss Cowen offered him a coy smile. "It is not every day that I am able to entertain a son of an earl in my home."

Elinor glanced at the door. "Will your mother be joining us?"

"No, she went to the apothecary to buy me some powder for this terrible headache I have," Miss Cowen said.

"I'm sorry that ails you," Alden remarked.

Miss Cowen brought a hand up to her forehead, her smile dimming. "I am afraid I suffer many afflictions, but I have had the strength to overcome each and every one of them. Some people consider me brave for all the trials that I must endure."

Alden didn't quite know what to say to that remark, so he remained quiet.

Fortunately, Elinor spoke up, drawing the attention away from him. "It is true," she said. "Maisie has endured many illnesses and has shown remarkable resilience in overcoming them."

Miss Cowen waved a dismissive hand in front of her. "Enough talk of me. I want to learn more about Mr. Dandridge." She patted the seat next to her on the settee. "Come sit by me. We have much to discuss."

With great reluctance, Alden approached the proffered chair and sat down. "What would you care to know?"

Leaning towards him, Miss Cowen said, "Your eyes are so blue. They remind me of the Loch Ness."

"Thank you," Alden responded, feeling uncomfortable by how close Miss Cowen was to him.

Elinor went to sit across from them. "I do not believe Mr. Dandridge has been to Loch Ness."

"We must go!" Miss Cowen urged. "The Loch Ness is

extraordinary. We could take a rowboat and spend hours on the lake."

Alden exchanged a glance with Elinor before asking, "Isn't it rather cold to go on the lake right now?"

"We could always remain close to one another to stay warm," Miss Cowen said, inching even closer to him.

He abruptly rose and walked to the mantel that hung over the hearth. "I'm afraid I do not have any intention of remaining in Scotland for too long."

Miss Cowen pouted. "That is a shame."

"Mr. Dandridge is only here long enough to find a wife before he returns to England," Elinor explained.

The pout on Miss Cowen's face disappeared. "I would make an excellent wife," she declared. "I have been preparing my whole life to be one."

Alden cleared his throat. "Wonderful," he muttered. What did one say to such a ridiculous remark?

Miss Cowen rose gracefully and began to dance around the room. "I am an excellent dancer. My dancing master told me that I glide across the floor quite nicely." She came to a stop in front of Alden. "And I can sing."

As she opened her mouth, presumably to sing a song, Alden quickly interjected. "That won't be necessary. I believe you."

Miss Cowen smoothed down her simple blue gown. "My mother encouraged my education so I wouldn't be a bore in the drawing room… or any other place, for that matter." She batted her eyelashes at him, her gaze unwavering.

Dear heavens, he needed a drink. His eyes darted around the room, searching desperately for a drink cart, but there was none in sight.

Elinor gave her friend a disapproving shake of her head. "Maisie… you know your mother would not approve of you saying such a thing."

"It is true," Miss Cowen said, her eyes still fixed on Alden.

"My mother is quite the prude, but I have read many books on the subject."

Alden turned his attention to Elinor, silently pleading for her help. He had no desire to marry someone that was so bold in their intentions.

Elinor must have understood what he was trying to convey because she rose. "I forgot that I promised Mr. Dandridge that we would go over the ledgers today."

"Ledgers?" Miss Cowen repeated, her expression turning to one of disappointment. "But that is so boring. Why not stay here and we can play a game of chess? I am quite good at it. Everyone has told me so."

"As tempting as that sounds..." Elinor started.

Miss Cowen spoke over her. "We could always go on a walk or have a cup of tea?" she asked eagerly. Too eagerly.

Alden decided it was best to intercede. "I do thank you for your hospitality, but we really do need to go."

"Fine," Miss Cowen responded, tossing her hands up in the air. "I have a headache anyways and I need to rest."

"I do hope you don't take offense—" Alden began.

Miss Cowen dropped down onto the settee. "I will be all right. You may go now." She laid back and placed a pillow over her face.

Alden went to say something, but Elinor put her hand up to stop him. "I shall call upon you again, Maisie."

"Don't bother. I shall probably be dead the next time you see me," Miss Cowen declared from beneath the pillow.

"You are not going to die," Elinor reassured her gently.

Miss Cowen removed the pillow from her face and looked up at Elinor. "How would you know? You are not a doctor."

Elinor smiled. "I am not, but I wish you well."

"Thank you for stopping by," Miss Cowen said, returning the pillow to her face with a sigh.

As Alden led Elinor from the manor, he asked, "Is Miss Cowen always like this?"

"She is not at her finest, I'm afraid," Elinor replied. "But that is one of the many reasons why I just adore her. She is rather entertaining."

"That could be a word for it," Alden muttered.

Once Elinor and her lady's maid were situated in the coach, Alden positioned himself across from them. "I find that women in Scotland are much more brazen than their English counterparts."

"You seem to forget that it is not common for the son of an English earl to be looking for a Scottish wife in this small village," Elinor pointed out. "But now that you have met all three ladies, is there one that strikes your fancy the most?"

This was it. Alden knew he had to lie in an attempt to make Elinor jealous. Would this ruse even work? "I suppose if I had to pick, I would pick Miss Cowen."

Elinor furrowed her brows. "Miss Cowen?" she repeated. "As in the young woman we just visited?"

"Yes, I do think she was quite lovely," he lied.

"Miss Cowen?" she echoed, her tone incredulous.

"Yes, Miss Cowen."

She stared at him in disbelief. "You would marry Miss Cowen?"

Alden reached up and rubbed his chin, pretending to consider his words carefully. "She is quite beautiful, and I do believe the doctors in England could help with her headaches," he said. "She is precisely what I am looking for in a young woman. She can dance, sing and I find many things intriguing about her."

Elinor pursed her lips. "Like what?"

He resisted the urge to chuckle, especially since he now had to come up with one thing he found intriguing about Miss Cowen. Was there anything? "She is clearly well-read, and I would like to get her opinion on a myriad of things. Further-more, she is very entertaining, and I appreciate her straight-forward manner, especially her promise of not being a bore."

"But it is Maisie," Elinor said. "She is…" Her words trailed off.

"She is what?" he prodded.

Elinor brought a smile to her lips. "She is… wonderful," she said through clenched teeth. "I hope you two are truly happy with one another."

"We will be," Alden responded.

"Good," Elinor muttered before she turned her attention to the window, retreating to her own thoughts.

Alden had no desire to ever marry Miss Cowen, but he wasn't about to tell Elinor that. If he didn't know any better, it almost seemed that Elinor was indeed jealous of Miss Cowen. He could only hope that might change her mind about marrying him.

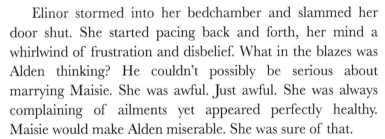

Elinor stormed into her bedchamber and slammed her door shut. She started pacing back and forth, her mind a whirlwind of frustration and disbelief. What in the blazes was Alden thinking? He couldn't possibly be serious about marrying Maisie. She was awful. Just awful. She was always complaining of ailments yet appeared perfectly healthy. Maisie would make Alden miserable. She was sure of that.

Drats. Why had she introduced him to Maisie? She should have just stopped with Gwendolyn and Isobel. Was Alden that desperate that he would truly consider Maisie?

A knock came at the door, and her aunt stepped in, concern etched on her face. "Is everything all right?"

"No!" Elinor shouted, tossing her hands up in exasperation. "Alden is going to marry Maisie."

"Maisie?"

"Yes, Maisie Cowen," Elinor confirmed.

Her aunt furrowed her brow. "Has he met Maisie?"

"Yes, we just went to call upon her, and Alden left being intrigued by her," Elinor shared. "Can you imagine that?"

Coming to sit on the settee, her aunt said, "I will admit that I did not see this coming, considering Maisie is rather difficult to please."

Elinor stopped pacing and turned to face her aunt. "Alden can't marry Maisie. She would make him miserable."

"Alden?"

Elinor pressed her lips together. "Yes, he gave me leave to call him by his given name."

"And you did the same?"

"I did," Elinor confirmed. "We are friends."

Her aunt looked at her curiously. "When did you become friends with Mr. Dandridge?" she asked.

"It is all about the ruse," Elinor said.

"Is it now?" her aunt asked, not quite looking convinced.

Elinor resumed her pacing. "I had to convince him that we are friends so he would trust me."

"There are rules to the ruse?"

"Of course," Elinor replied. "But if he marries Maisie, I have lost. He will sell the horse farm and we will have nowhere to go."

Her aunt rose and approached her. "First things first, you have not lost. And now is not the time to give up."

Elinor faced her aunt. "What am I to do?"

"You are asking me?" her aunt asked. "You must be desperate."

"I can't lose this horse farm."

Her aunt tapped her lips thoughtfully. "I wonder if there is something you could do to convince him not to sell the horse farm."

Elinor's shoulders slumped. "I have tried, but he is adamant that he wants to sell it to buy land in England."

"What if you married him?" her aunt asked.

She reared back. "Have you lost your senses? He wants a marriage of convenience and I want—"

Her aunt spoke over her. "Love," she said. "I know, but I do think it is possible for you two to get what you both want."

"And how do we go about doing that?"

With a slight shrug, her aunt said, "You two just need to fall madly in love with one another."

Elinor huffed. "I do believe playing the bagpipes has caused you to spout nonsense."

"Hear me out," her aunt said. "You like him, he likes you…"

"No," Elinor said with a shake of her head. "I don't like him. I can barely tolerate him, and he is going to marry Maisie. It is over."

"All right," her aunt conceded, taking a step back.

Elinor lifted her brow. "That is all you have to say?"

"What else can I say?" her aunt asked. "If you aren't interested in Mr. Dandridge, there is no point in pursuing him."

"I'm not," Elinor lied.

"Very well," her aunt said, walking over to the door. "Not that you are interested, but I do believe Mr. Dandridge is still in the library."

"Well, I do not care where Mr. Dandridge spends his time," Elinor said.

Her aunt smiled, as if she had found her words to be amusing. "Then I shall see you for supper."

Once her aunt had left, it only took Elinor a moment before she knew her aunt was right. She was interested in Mr. Dandridge, which only seemed to irk her more. And she wanted to see him.

Elinor approached the mirror and smoothed back her dark hair before she headed out the door. With quick steps, she approached the library.

This was madness.

She should turn around and go back to her bedchamber. But she couldn't convince herself to do so.

Stepping into the library, she saw Alden was sitting down, a book in his hand. He glanced up and promptly rose when he saw her. "Elinor," he greeted. "I thought you were going to rest."

"I was," Elinor said as she walked closer to him. "But I… uh… wanted a book to read. I had no idea that you would be in here."

Alden smiled and she felt the familiar fluttering in her stomach. "Perhaps I can help you select a book."

Elinor pointed towards the book in his hand. "May I ask what you are reading?"

Holding the book up, he replied, "It is a book of sonnets by William Shakespeare."

"How intriguing."

"Truly?" Alden asked.

She shook her head. "No, I prefer Shakespeare's plays to his sonnets," she responded. "I am surprised you didn't select a book that was written in Latin."

Alden put the book down onto the table and looked at Elinor with a solemn look. "Can I tell you a secret?"

"Always," Elinor replied, her curiosity piqued.

"I studied Latin at university because I wanted to eventually become a barrister," Alden shared.

Elinor cocked her head. "And now?"

Alden grinned. "As you can see, I am not a barrister," he replied. "I applied to Lincoln's Inn and got accepted."

"Then what happened?"

"I studied with barristers and shared many meals with them," Alden said. "But I wasn't passionate about it. It didn't make me happy."

Elinor took a step closer to him. "What does make you happy?"

Alden winced, looking away briefly before meeting her gaze again. "I want to be a landowner in England."

"Why does it have to be in England?" Elinor asked. "Why can't you be happy with owning land in Scotland?"

"Scotland is not my home," Alden said.

Elinor met his gaze. "It could be," she argued. "You could get married and start off with a successful horse farm."

Alden looked at her like she was mad. "I know nothing about horses."

"But I do," Elinor asserted. "I could continue to run it and you could—"

"Do what? Sit around and twiddle my thumbs?" Alden asked, a hint of frustration in his voice.

Elinor forced a smile to her lips. "I can teach you everything I know and then you could eventually run it."

Alden moved to stand in front of her, his proximity making her heart race. "What will you do then?"

"I am rather resourceful," Elinor responded. "I could find something else to do. You wouldn't need to worry about me."

"But I do worry about you, Elinor," Alden said softly.

Elinor bit her lower lip, her emotions a tangled mess. "You shouldn't since you are going to marry Maisie," she said, her voice barely above a whisper.

Alden brought his hand up and gently tucked a piece of errant hair behind her ear. "Is there a reason why you don't think I should marry Miss Cowen?"

Yes.

She had many reasons, but she couldn't seem to find the strength to say one. Not when he was standing this close to her.

He leaned closer. "Do you want to know what I think?"

She nodded, her eyes dropping to his lips.

"I think you might be jealous that I am showing interest in Miss Cowen," Alden whispered.

Elinor's eyes snapped up. "Jealous?" she repeated, her

voice incredulous. "Why would I be jealous? I am the farthest thing from being jealous."

Alden looked amused. "Your actions tell me otherwise."

"No. If anything, I am happy for you," Elinor said with a defiant tilt of her chin. "I hope you and Miss Cowen have a horde of children."

"Is that so?" Alden asked.

Elinor bobbed her head. "Yes, and for you to suggest otherwise is ludicrous. I think you and Miss Cowen are perfect for one another."

Alden brought his hand up and ran his finger down the length of her cheek, sending shivers down her spine. "Yet you have made no effort to distance yourself from me."

"Need I remind you that you approached me, not the other way around?" Elinor asked, struggling to keep her voice steady.

His lips quirked into a half-smile. "Why won't you admit that you have some feelings for me?"

"When pigs fly," Elinor retorted.

Alden leaned forward until their lips were just inches apart and asked, "Do you want to kiss me, Elinor?"

Yes.

It would be so easy to go up on her tiptoes and press her lips against his. But what would that accomplish?

As her heart pounded in her chest, the sound of the main door being slammed echoed throughout the manor, followed by a booming voice calling, "Elinor!"

Elinor stepped out of Alden's comforting arms, and she felt dread washing over her. How she wished she never had to hear that voice again.

"What is wrong?" Alden asked.

She glanced over her shoulder at the doorway, her face paling. "It is my uncle," she said. "He has come to take me home."

Chapter Twelve

Alden could see the color drain from Elinor's face, and the panic was evident in her trembling voice. He stepped closer and gently took her hand in his. "It will be all right," he encouraged, his voice steady and calm.

She shook her head vigorously. "No, it won't be," she insisted. "My uncle is a man that is used to getting what he wants."

"Then he has met his match in you," Alden responded.

Elinor offered him a weak smile, but it didn't reach her eyes. "You are kind to say so, but it is utterly untrue. Uncle Matthew can be very persuasive when he wants to be."

Alden tightened his hold on her hand, his resolve unyielding. "Would you like me to go with you?"

Elinor's eyes flickered with uncertainty. "I would, but I am not sure if that is the best idea," she responded. "My uncle will no doubt turn his ire onto you."

"Better than you," Alden stated firmly.

The echo of her uncle's angry voice reverberated through the manor. "Elinor!" he bellowed.

Elinor glanced anxiously at the doorway. "It is better if I do this alone."

"Why?" he asked, his eyes searching hers for an answer.

She met his gaze, her expression resolute. "This is not your fight."

"Perhaps not, but we are friends," he asserted. "And friends help one another."

"But Uncle Matthew…" she began, her voice faltering.

Alden brought their hands up to his lips. "Has no true power over you. You have reached your majority."

"He threatened to send me to an asylum if I didn't marry the duke," Elinor admitted with a slight wince.

"I won't let that happen," Alden assured her.

Just then, a maid hurried into the room, her face lighting up with relief upon seeing Elinor. "Your uncle, the Marquess of Inglewood, is requesting a moment of your time, Miss."

Alden's brow shot up in disbelief. "Your uncle is Lord Inglewood?"

"He is," Elinor confirmed. "Uncle Matthew inherited the title after my father died."

Lowering their entwined hands, Alden said, "That means I should have been addressing you as Lady Elinor this whole time."

"No," Elinor responded firmly. "I left that life behind me when I refused to marry the duke. I am just Elinor now."

"And your aunt allowed this?"

"Yes, she understood the reasons as to why I dropped my title," Elinor responded. "I didn't want my uncle to find me in Scotland."

"Does your household staff know the truth?"

"Only Bryon knows who I truly am," Elinor responded.

Alden didn't know what to feel at this precise moment. Not only did Elinor outrank him, but she had also kept this significant part of her life from him.

The maid cleared her throat politely, reminding them that they were not alone. "My lady, your uncle is waiting for you."

Elinor nodded in acknowledgement. "Please inform him I will be down in a moment."

With a brief curtsy, the maid departed to do her bidding.

Turning back towards Alden, Elinor said, "You don't have to come with me. I can do this on my own."

"You can, but you don't have to," Alden responded. "I will accompany you."

Elinor glanced down at their joined hands. "I'm sorry I lied to you, but I was hiding from my uncle. I couldn't risk anyone knowing the truth," she said softly. "I am not quite sure how he found me."

"That is neither here nor there. Let us go down and face your uncle together," Alden encouraged, offering her a reassuring smile.

"Together," Elinor repeated.

As Alden led her from the library, he noticed how visibly tense she was. "It will be all right," he said.

"You don't know my uncle," Elinor replied, her voice trembling.

"Actually, I do know him," he said. "I studied under him to be a barrister. He was one of the reasons why I decided not to pursue that profession."

Elinor looked at him in surprise. "I heard he was a shrewd barrister."

"You could say that," Alden said. "I didn't agree with his methods, and we had a falling out because of it."

Once they reached the top step of the stairs, Alden could see Lord Inglewood standing imposingly in the entry hall below. His nostrils flared with anger, and his dark, piercing eyes locked on to them. He was a tall man with a stern countenance, his presence always commanding respect and fear, traits that were well-established long before he inherited the title of marquess.

Lord Inglewood scoffed, and his voice dripped with

disdain. "It is about time you graced me with your presence, Niece."

Elinor slipped her hand out of Alden's as they descended the stairs. "I had not expected you this evening," she said, her voice steady. "Will you join us for supper?"

"No, I came to see you home," Lord Inglewood growled, his words more of a command than a statement.

"I am home," Elinor asserted, a flicker of defiance in her eyes.

Lord Inglewood's gaze shifted to Alden, his eyes narrowing suspiciously. "What are you doing here, Mr. Dandridge?"

Alden stood his ground. "My reasons are my own."

Lord Inglewood's eyes darted between Alden and Elinor, suspicion etched into his features. "What is going on between you two?"

"Nothing. We are just friends," Elinor said quickly. "Mr. Dandridge is Lady Edith's great-nephew and has come to see the horse farm."

Lord Inglewood's expression remained unconvinced, but he chose not to press the issue. "Go pack your trunks and we will be off," he ordered.

Elinor tilted her chin. "No," she replied firmly.

"No?" Lord Inglewood repeated, his voice rising with incredulity. "You seem to forget that you are my ward."

"Not since I have reached my majority," Elinor said, her voice firm. "I am free to do as I please."

"With what funds?" Lord Inglewood sneered.

Elinor clasped her hands in front of her. "I am running this horse farm for Lady Edith," she shared.

Lord Inglewood's mouth dropped. "You are working like a common laborer. Are you mad?" he asked. "You are a lady."

"That is my past," Elinor responded resolutely.

"You can't run from your past," Lord Inglewood said, his voice harsh. "Furthermore, the Duke of Mardale is still willing to marry you. You could be a duchess, not a horse farmer."

Elinor pressed her lips together. "Be that as it may, I choose to remain here and run the horse farm."

"You cannot be in earnest!" Lord Inglewood exclaimed, his face contorted with anger.

"I am," Elinor responded.

Lord Inglewood took a menacing step closer to Elinor, and she stepped back, fear flickering in her eyes. "I am done with your tantrum. It is time to go home," he said, his voice low and threatening.

Alden stepped forward, placing himself protectively between Elinor and her uncle. "She is home, Lord Inglewood," he stated.

Mrs. Hardy's voice came from the corridor. "Lord Inglewood," she greeted, her steps quickening as she approached. "What a pleasant surprise. What brings you to Scotland?"

With a clenched jaw and a hint of disdain, Lord Inglewood muttered, "Mrs. Hardy."

Mrs. Hardy came to a stop by Elinor. "I was just informed that supper is ready. Would you care to join us this evening?"

"I would prefer to leave this wretched place and return home," Lord Inglewood grumbled, his voice laden with irritation.

"Go on, then," Mrs. Hardy responded, gesturing towards the door. "No one is stopping you from leaving."

Lord Inglewood turned his heated glare to Elinor. "I am not leaving without my niece."

"Then you will be leaving disappointed," Mrs. Hardy said. "Lady Elinor is not going anywhere with you."

"We shall see," Lord Inglewood stated.

Mrs. Hardy and Lord Inglewood stood face to face, the tension between them almost tangible. Their silent battle of wills stretched on, the air thick with unspoken threats. Finally, after a long moment, Lord Inglewood conceded with a huff. "I shall join you for dinner, considering the late hour."

"Wonderful," Mrs. Hardy said, her voice taking on a

cheery lilt. "Let us try to have a pleasant conversation for once."

Alden offered his arm to Elinor. "May I escort you to the dining room?" he asked.

Elinor accepted his arm and kept her head held high. Though he had known her for only a short time, Alden recognized the brave front she was putting on, and he hoped her courage was not solely for his benefit.

He patted her hand. "It will be all right," he whispered.

"I wish I had your confidence."

Leaning closer, he said, "You are stronger than you think you are. Just remember that."

Elinor met his gaze. "You are kind to say that."

"It is merely the truth," he said. "Don't give your uncle any more power than he already has."

"You are right," Elinor said, her voice gaining strength.

Alden smirked. "I usually am. It is what makes me so charming."

A laugh escaped Elinor's lips. "You are vexing," she said lightly.

"But not charming?" he prompted.

"No, more vexing," Elinor quipped, a glint of mirth in her eyes.

Lord Inglewood's curt voice cut through their exchange. "Is something amusing, Elinor?" he asked.

The humor drained from Elinor's expression. "No, Uncle," she replied, her voice much more subdued.

After they stepped into the dining room, Alden pulled out a chair for Elinor. He knew this was going to be a long, and no doubt tedious, dinner, but there was no other place he would rather be.

Elinor tried to pretend that her uncle's intense glares didn't bother her, but they did. How in the blazes had he found her? She had been so careful to hide herself away in Scotland. When his letters had first arrived, she had been surprised but never truly believed he would travel all this way to retrieve her in person.

Not that she had any intention of going anywhere with him. She refused to return home and marry the Duke of Mardale. The mere thought of the old duke, with his gouty bandaged feet, made her shudder. She didn't care that he was a duke.

She glanced at Alden, grateful for his steadying presence beside her. She had thought herself brave enough to face her uncle alone, but she had been wrong. She needed Alden by her side more than she realized.

The footmen stepped forward, placing bowls of steaming soup in front of them. From his place at the head of the table, Lord Inglewood picked up his spoon and took a sip. "This isn't awful," he remarked with grudging approval before placing the spoon back down.

Her aunt spoke up. "I shall inform the cook of your praise," she said dryly.

Uncle Matthew met Aunt Cecilia's gaze. "Why are you here?"

With a slight shrug of her shoulders, Aunt Cecilia replied, "I could ask you the same thing, my lord."

"I am her guardian," her uncle snapped.

"I do believe Elinor no longer requires a guardian, especially given the fine job you did," Aunt Cecilia retorted.

Uncle Matthew glared at her. "I must assume I have you to thank for her running away at the chapel."

Elinor spoke up, her voice determined. "No, I chose to do that on my own."

"And what a foolish mistake that was," her uncle said.

"Fortunately, the duke understands that you simply had cold feet and is still willing to marry you."

"I do not wish to marry him," Elinor responded.

"You would be a duchess," her uncle argued, leaning forward.

Elinor shook her head. "The duke only wants to marry me because he wants an heir. Any young woman would do."

"No, you caught the duke's eye, and he is very interested in furthering your acquaintance," her uncle said.

"I won't do it," Elinor asserted.

"Then I shall remain here until you do change your mind," her uncle stated.

Aunt Cecilia picked up a roll and tossed it at Lord Inglewood, the bread hitting him squarely on the shoulder. "My apologies, my lord. It must have slipped," she said, her tone devoid of any genuine regret.

Her uncle brushed off the crumbs on his jacket, his expression one of barely contained irritation. "Truly?" he asked. "Is this the example you wish to set for Lady Elinor?"

"I do believe she is doing just fine," Aunt Cecilia said.

"She is wasting her life by running a horse farm," her uncle countered sharply. "She should be running a large household as a duchess."

Aunt Cecilia sighed, a deep and weary sound. "She doesn't want to be a duchess. Why can't you seem to get that through your thick head?"

Her uncle tsked. "Name calling now? I would expect better from you."

Elinor glanced at Alden, who was watching her intently. When their eyes met, he winked, providing her with much needed reassurance. She felt a small surge of courage from his silent support.

Reaching for his glass, her uncle continued. "I should have known that Lady Edith would have helped you. She is an eccentric old bat."

"Do not talk that way about Lady Edith," Elinor asserted. "I turned to her when no one else would help me."

"That is because everyone knew what a great opportunity it was for you to marry a duke," her uncle responded. "Well, everyone but you, apparently."

Elinor frowned. "I wanted to marry for love."

"Love?" Her uncle slammed his glass down onto the table, causing water to spill over his hand. "Love is for poor people. Simpletons. Not ladies of genteel birth."

"My parents loved each other very much," Elinor responded.

Her uncle wiped his hand with a napkin. "Give it time. They would have eventually grown to hate one another."

Elinor's frown deepened. "You know not what you speak of."

"Neither do you," her uncle stated. "You are young, foolish, naive—"

Alden interrupted, his voice calm but firm. "You are wrong," he said. "Lady Elinor is none of those things."

Her uncle turned his heated glare to Alden. "And how exactly would you know that?" he demanded.

"I have become acquainted with Lady Elinor over these past few days—"

"How acquainted?" her uncle asked, his tone insinuating.

Alden grew indignant. "Not in the way that you are implying," he declared.

Her uncle leaned back in his seat. "What am I supposed to think?" he asked. "I show up…"

"Uninvited, might I add," her aunt muttered under her breath

"… and you are cavorting with my niece," her uncle said, ignoring Cecilia's comment.

Alden's jaw clenched tightly. "We were not cavorting," he responded. "And I resent the implication."

"Were you not holding hands with my niece earlier, or did I just imagine that?" her uncle asked.

"I was offering comfort to Lady Elinor," Alden responded, his tone unwavering.

Her uncle arched an eyebrow. "Comfort?" he repeated. "Is that what you call it when you are too familiar with a young woman?"

Elinor had just about enough of her uncle. How dare he imply that anything inappropriate went on between them. "Uncle Matthew," she began, "you are wrong. Mr. Dandridge and I are just friends."

"Friends? No. I daresay that you two have been spending far too much time alone," her uncle said, shifting his gaze towards Aunt Cecilia. "It does not appear that Mrs. Hardy is a very good chaperone."

Her aunt smiled. "As usual, you are wrong in your assumptions."

"I don't think I am," her uncle said. "Does Lady Edith know what is going on under her roof?"

"Yes, she does," her aunt confirmed without hesitation.

Her uncle narrowed his eyes at Aunt Cecilia before turning his steely gaze back to Alden. "Have you told Elinor how you were not called up to the bar?" he asked.

"That was by choice," Alden shot back.

Her uncle huffed. "Was it?" he asked, leaning forward in his seat. "I recall it quite differently."

"You would be wrong," Alden contended.

Addressing Elinor, her uncle revealed with a smug grin, "Mr. Dandridge could not seem to hack it as a barrister. He failed time and time again."

"I doubt that to be true," she replied.

"Well, you would be wrong, as usual," her uncle said. "It became rather evident that Mr. Dandridge is not as clever as he thinks he is."

Elinor didn't believe a single word out of her uncle's

mouth. She knew he had a habit of lying whenever it suited him. Besides, she had come to know Alden well. He was clever and kind, traits her uncle sorely lacked.

"You are right, Uncle," Elinor said, her voice steady. "Mr. Dandridge is not as clever as he thinks he is."

Her uncle's face lit up with a triumphant smile.

But Elinor wasn't done. She continued, "He is smarter."

The smile vanished from her uncle's lips, replaced by a sneer. "I see that he has you fooled."

As the footmen stepped forward to retrieve the soup bowls and place the main courses before them, Elinor turned to Alden, concerned about the impact of her uncle's words. "Do not let my uncle's words get to you," she whispered. "They are only just that... words."

Alden tipped his head slightly, acknowledging her words, but she could see the fury simmering in his eyes.

Her uncle began eating and asked, "Is there a guest bedchamber in this incessant manor?"

"There is room in the stables with the other animals," her aunt remarked with a smile.

Elinor interjected, "There is a guest bedchamber available."

"Good," her uncle replied. "Since tonight is Christmas Eve, we should celebrate. Have the candles been lit?"

Bryon stepped forward and announced, "They have been, my lord, and will continue to burn through Christmas."

Her uncle waved the butler back with a flick of his hand. "Well, at least your household has managed that. It is a shame that you don't have a Yule log."

"We are attending Christmas service tomorrow at our local parish," her aunt informed Lord Inglewood. "I would imagine you won't be accompanying us to prevent the church from being struck by lightning."

With a glance heavenward, her uncle said, "I would rather sleep in than attend church with you."

"Well, if that is the case, I hope you feel the same way about our Christmas feast," her aunt responded.

Elinor resisted the urge to smile at her aunt's jabs at her uncle. Everyone was thinking it, but she was the only one brave enough to say it.

Her uncle held up his glass to Aunt Cecilia and said, "As usual, it is a delight being around you," he mocked.

Aunt Cecilia simply smiled back. "The feeling is mutual, my lord."

Chapter Thirteen

Alden stared out the window of his bedchamber, watching the snow gently blanket the fields. Today was Christmas. He had every reason to celebrate but his thoughts kept turning to Elinor. She had managed to bewitch him, and now his heart was turning towards hers. A heart that was supposed to be impenetrable.

The door creaked open and Hastings stepped into the room. "Good morning, sir," he greeted.

"Good morning," Alden muttered, his gaze still fixed on the falling snow.

Hastings approached the wardrobe, selecting Alden's attire for the day. "The coach should be arriving soon to take you to the church."

"Wonderful," Alden said, his tone flat.

After Hastings removed the clothing from the wardrobe, he placed them on the bed. "I do believe a green jacket and a red waistcoat would be most festive today. What do you think?"

Alden shrugged. "I care little about that."

"Is there something on your mind, sir?" Hastings asked.

Turning to meet his valet's gaze, Alden asked, "Why can't women be more predictable?"

Hastings responded with an understanding smile. "If that was the case, life would be very boring. I take it this is about Lady Elinor."

"It is. She is maddening," Alden said as he walked over to the bed.

"Women usually are, especially when you have feelings for them," Hastings remarked knowingly.

Alden shifted uncomfortably. "I may have some feelings for her, but that is not what is important."

"Of course it is important," Hastings countered. "And I do believe your feelings are much deeper than you care to admit."

"No, that is impossible. Women love me, not the other way around," Alden remarked.

Hastings grinned. "Is it possible that you have finally met your match?"

As Alden started dressing, he grew quiet. Was Elinor his match? No, that could not be. He wanted to marry her only because he wanted this horse farm. Yet, the thought of waking up next to her every morning held an undeniable appeal.

Botheration.

Hastings was right. He cared deeply for Elinor. But love? That was impossible. He couldn't- no, he wouldn't- fall in love with Elinor.

Hastings stepped forward, offering Alden the cravat. "With all due respect, I do believe your silence speaks volumes."

Alden accepted the cravat, tying it with a deft hand. "You may be right," he admitted. "I care for Elinor, but I won't fall in love with her."

"I never said anything about love, sir," Hastings pointed out.

"Good, because it is foolish to even think about such a thing," Alden responded.

Hastings tipped his head in agreement. "However, what do you intend to do with the horse farm if you convince Lady Elinor to marry you?"

Alden frowned. "I want to sell it, but I suspect Elinor wouldn't marry me if I did such a thing."

"Most likely," Hastings said, "and Scotland is growing on me."

No truer words had ever been said. When Alden had first arrived, he couldn't wait to leave this blasted country, but now he found the horse farm a reprieve from life, just as Elinor had. What was happening to him? He had a plan. But his plan was shifting, and it was all because of Elinor.

Alden walked over to the mirror and adjusted his cravat. "Regardless, I am not quite sure I can convince Elinor to marry me since she wants love," he admitted, his voice tinged with frustration.

Hastings looked amused. "I am sure you will find a way."

"I wish I had your optimism," Alden sighed.

A knock at the door interrupted their conversation and Hastings crossed the room to answer it. A footman stood there, announcing, "The coach is out front, sir. The driver is ready to take you to the church."

"Thank you," Alden acknowledged, casting one last critical glance at his reflection. Everything was in place, but he couldn't help wondering if Elinor would find him lacking.

Once the footman departed, Hastings held the door open for Alden. "If I may be so bold, I have noticed how happy you seem lately. I suspect it has much to do with Lady Elinor."

Alden nodded, a small smile playing at his lips. "You are right," he admitted. "Elinor does make me immensely happy-far happier than I have ever been."

Hastings lowered his voice. "I have heard rumors from the

servants at the manor that say you have almost kissed Lady Elinor on multiple occasions."

"Yes, that is true," Alden admitted as he approached the door. "But I won't kiss her unless she is truly ready. I am attempting to be a gentleman."

"Well, Christmas is a day of miracles, sir," Hastings remarked.

Alden chuckled, a genuine warmth spreading through him. "For the first time, in a long time, I find that I suspect I am going to enjoy this holiday."

Hastings smiled. "I wish you luck, sir."

As Alden approached his door, a thought occurred to him. He stopped and turned to face his valet. "I am sorry that I took you away from your wife on Christmas."

"I am most fortunate to have a very understanding wife," Hastings said with a reflective look in his eyes. "We will celebrate once I return home."

"I do appreciate all that you do for me," Alden remarked.

Hastings tipped his head in acknowledgement. "It has been a pleasure to serve you, sir, and I hope you find what you seek. Now, you must hurry if you don't want to be late for the church service."

Once Alden departed from his bedchamber, he made his way to the awaiting coach. He settled back into his seat and watched the snow create a picturesque white wonderland outside the window. The snowflakes clung to the ground, and he found himself smiling at the serene beauty of it all.

He could be happy here. With Elinor. In truth, he could be happy anywhere as long as she was by his side. He just wanted to be with her.

And then the realization struck him like a bolt of lightning.

He was halfway in love with her.

Good gads! What had he done? Had he not just resolved

to not fall in love? Love would complicate a marriage between them, and he didn't need any more complications in his life.

The coach came to a stop in front of a quaint stone church, and he watched as the parishioners filed inside.

His mind churned with emotions. What was he going to do? He couldn't possibly admit such feelings to Elinor, not when they were likely unrequited. He couldn't even convince her to kiss him, let alone marry him.

But then he saw her. Elinor stepped gracefully out of a coach, dressed in a pale green gown that accentuated her delicate features. Her hair was styled in an elegant chignon, and her cheeks were flushed a rosy pink from the morning chill. She looked every bit the enchanting vision that had captivated his heart.

In that moment, he knew everything would be all right. When he was around Elinor, he felt calm, at peace. She allowed him to be who he truly was, not the persona he adopted to fit into high Society.

Alden departed the coach and approached her. "Good morning, Lady Elinor," he greeted with a warm smile.

"Good morning," she responded, her eyes lighting up at the sight of him. Or had he just imagined that? He hoped not.

He stopped in front of her, being mindful to maintain a proper distance. "I trust that you slept well."

A slight furrow appeared between her brows. "I did not go to bed until late. My uncle was relentless in trying to convince me to marry the duke," she shared with a weary sigh.

"I'm sorry," Alden responded, his heart aching for her. "I can only imagine how difficult that must have been.

"It matters not since I refuse to marry the duke and be added to his collection of fine things," Elinor remarked.

"I think you are wise to do so."

"My uncle says I am stupid to pass on such an advantageous marriage," Elinor shared.

Alden smirked. "Well, if I may say, your uncle is a mutton-head," he responded.

Elinor laughed, and the sound was like music to his soul. "I couldn't agree more," she said. "Although, I am sorry he said such hurtful things about you last night during supper."

"It is all right. I have come to see that Lord Inglewood and I will never see eye to eye on most things," Alden remarked.

"I do believe that is a good thing," Elinor retorted with a wry smile.

Alden glanced over her shoulder before revealing, "Your uncle was right about one thing, though. I couldn't hack being a barrister."

"That can't be true..."

He cut her off gently. "No, it is true," he said. "I just wanted to uphold the law and defend my clients. Unfortunately, there are a lot of politics that go hand in hand with being a barrister, and I refused to play that game."

Elinor bobbed her head in understanding. "Then you made the right choice. You must do what your conscience dictates."

"Your uncle doesn't see it that way," Alden pointed out.

"Well, as you said so yourself, my uncle is a muttonhead," Elinor said, her eyes twinkling with amusement. "I tend to disregard most of what he says."

Alden offered his arm. "May I escort you inside for the service?"

"I would greatly appreciate that," she replied, taking his arm.

As they entered the church, Alden saw that it was crowded, but he managed to find two seats in a pew near the back. They were just settling in when a familiar voice called out, "Mr. Dandridge!"

Alden turned to see Mrs. MacBain waving at him from the front of the church. He tipped his head in acknowledgement, hoping that was the end of it. Unfortunately, he was not so lucky.

Mrs. MacBain rose and walked around the pews to stand next to him. "I hope you are having a fine Christmas."

"I am," he replied. "And you?"

She batted her eyelashes at him. "I hope that you might find the time to come to call upon me today."

"I... uh..." he started, struggling to find a polite way to decline.

Elinor spoke up. "Unfortunately, today will be rather busy since my uncle is in town and we are having a Christmas feast."

Mrs. MacBain's face fell. "Tomorrow, then?"

Fortunately, the vicar walked to the front of the room, indicating the service was about to begin. With a slight curtsy, Mrs. MacBain returned to her seat.

Leaning closer to Elinor, Alden said in a hushed voice, "Thank you."

She playfully nudged his shoulder with hers. "It is the least I could do, considering it is Christmas," she said. "Now, do try to listen to the service. You might learn something."

Alden tried to focus on the vicar's words, but the scent of lavender drifting from Elinor made it difficult. How could he concentrate on anything else when all he wanted was to pull her into his arms and kiss her?

Blazes.

This was going to be a long service.

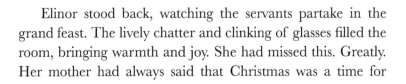

Elinor stood back, watching the servants partake in the grand feast. The lively chatter and clinking of glasses filled the room, bringing warmth and joy. She had missed this. Greatly. Her mother had always said that Christmas was a time for others, but Elinor had been so focused on herself lately that she had forgotten what truly mattered.

Her gaze drifted to Alden, who was mingling with the servants, looking entirely too dashing for his own good. She was in trouble. The more time she spent with Alden, the more her heart turned towards him. Not that she wanted to fall for anyone. No. She was doing just fine on her own.

But she knew that wasn't true.

She loved running a horse farm, but she wanted more. A husband. Children. And the worst part was, whenever she dreamed of having a family, her mind always conjured up the image of Alden.

Her aunt approached her with a drink in her hand. "Are you not hungry?"

"I was just woolgathering," Elinor admitted.

"Anything you wish to share?" her aunt asked, her eyes twinkling with curiosity.

Elinor shook her head. "No, it was just nonsensical stuff."

"Those are the best kind of thoughts," her aunt teased with a smile. "I haven't seen your uncle all day. With any luck, he will give up and pack his trunks."

"I do not think he will go so easily," Elinor remarked, her tone tinged with worry.

Her aunt frowned. "That is what I am worried about, as well," she said.

As if their words had summoned her uncle, he stepped into the room with Constable Gregor, who wore a solemn expression.

Her uncle closed the distance between them and said, "Let us speak privately about an urgent matter."

Aunt Cecilia stepped between them. "What urgent matter, my lord?" she asked. "And why is Constable Gregor here?"

His eyes flashed with annoyance. "It is none of your business, Woman. This is between Elinor and me."

Not wishing to cause a scene, Elinor spoke up. "We can speak in the drawing room," she said.

Her uncle took a step back and gestured towards the doorway. As she turned to leave, she caught Alden's eyes and she saw the questions deep within. She tilted her chin, encouraging him to join them. Whatever her uncle had to say to her, he could do so in front of Alden.

Elinor headed towards the drawing room and came to a stop in the center of the room. Alden stepped into the room and approached her. "What is going on?" he asked in a hushed voice.

She shrugged. "I don't know, but my uncle said he needed to speak to me about an urgent matter."

"On Christmas?" Alden asked, his brow furrowing.

Her uncle stepped into the room and narrowed his eyes at Alden. "You may leave, Mr. Dandridge. This does not concern you."

Elinor took a step closer to him. "I want him to stay."

Looking displeased, her uncle said, "Suit yourself."

Her aunt entered the room, her eyes immediately meeting Constable Gregor's gaze. "How is your family?" she asked.

The constable looked deucedly uncomfortable, shuffling his feet. "Aye, they're weel," he responded, his voice a low rumble.

Turning towards Lord Inglewood, her aunt's tone hardened. "Now, what is this all about, my lord?"

With a flourish, Lord Inglewood reached into his jacket pocket and pulled out two pieces of paper. "I have two doctors that have confirmed that my niece, Lady Elinor, is suffering from hysteria. Constable Gregor is here to ensure she is transported to an asylum."

Elinor reared back, disbelief etched across her face. "I beg your pardon?"

Aunt Cecilia moved to stand by Elinor, her expression

fierce. "This is ludicrous. Elinor wasn't even seen by a doctor. How could they make that determination?"

"She refused to marry the Duke of Mardale, which calls into question her sanity," her uncle said with a smug grin. "Unless she has since changed her mind?"

Elinor's mouth dropped. "You truly cannot be in earnest? You would force me to go to an asylum if I do not marry the duke."

Her uncle slipped the papers back into his jacket, his eyes cold. "Not me, but the doctors would," he contended. "Come with me and do try to avoid causing a scene."

Alden moved to stand in front of her, shielding her from her uncle. "Lady Elinor is not going anywhere with you. She is not mad."

"It is not up to you to decide, is it?" Lord Inglewood asked, his voice dripping with contempt. "As the closest male relation to her, it is my right to ensure she is not a danger to herself or others."

Aunt Cecilia turned her attention towards the constable, her voice pleading. "Gregor, please say that you are not going along with this."

The constable shrugged, his expression regretful. "Aye, I'm afraid I have nae choice."

"But Elinor isn't mad!" Aunt Cecilia shouted. "Lord Inglewood just wants to force her hand to marry a duke."

"All of his documentation is in order," the constable said. "If I dinnae take Lady Elinor, someone else will."

Alden spun around to face Elinor, his eyes intense. "Marry me," he whispered urgently.

"What?" she asked, her voice barely above a whisper. "You can't be in earnest."

"I am. It is the only way to protect you," Alden responded, his eyes searching hers.

Her eyes went wide. "Do you even want to marry me?"

"I do," he said quickly, his voice firm.

Elinor knew that she had to make a choice. She could marry Alden, knowing he would never love her, or go to an asylum until she would eventually be forced to marry the Duke of Mardale.

Her uncle's voice broke through her musings. "Come along, Elinor," he ordered. "Don't make this harder than it has to be."

"No," Elinor said, standing her ground. "I am not going with you. I am staying here… with Alden."

With a sigh, her uncle responded, "Constable. Retrieve my niece."

Alden reached for Elinor's hand and shifted to face Lord Inglewood. "I declare that I want Lady Elinor to be my wife."

Lord Inglewood looked heavenward, exasperation clear in his eyes. "My niece is mad. She cannot enter a marriage contract with you."

"In England, yes, but in Scotland they have something known as 'irregular marriages'," Alden informed him. "All Lady Elinor has to say is that she wants to be my wife, and we are married in the eyes of the law."

"Why would my niece want to marry you?" Lord Inglewood demanded. "You are nothing. A mere second son of an earl."

"That is true, but I refuse to let her be locked up in an asylum at your whim," Alden responded, his voice steady and resolute.

Aunt Cecilia met Elinor's gaze, her eyes holding compassion. "If you agree to marry Alden, your uncle will never have control over you again."

Elinor glanced down at their entwined hands, feeling the weight of the decision pressing on her. It was evident that her uncle would stop at nothing to ensure she married the duke, and the thought of being locked away in an asylum filled her with dread.

Her uncle snapped his fingers impatiently. "Elinor. Stop

this madness and come with me. You don't want to marry Mr. Dandridge."

"Why?" Elinor asked, her voice challenging.

Annoyance flickered in her uncle's eyes. "Don't throw your life away for the likes of Mr. Dandridge. You could be a duchess."

Elinor looked at her uncle in disbelief. "You are trying to throw me into an asylum to force my hand. Whereas Alden is trying to help me."

"Help you?" her uncle snapped. "He just wants your dowry. Don't be fooled by him."

Alden tightened his hold on her hand as he responded, "Your uncle is a liar. I didn't even know you had a dowry."

Her uncle tossed his hands in the air. "Of course she has a dowry, you daft man. She is the daughter of a marquess," he stated. "I have had just about enough of this conversation. Do your job, Constable."

As the constable took a step closer to her, Alden leaned in and said in a hushed voice, "Marry me, please."

Elinor knew she truly only had one choice. In a steady voice, she said, "I declare that I want to marry Mr. Dandridge."

"No!" her uncle exclaimed. "What did you do, you stupid chit?"

Constable Gregor took a step back, nodding solemnly. "Now that Lady Elinor is wed, her husband is who'll speak for her," he said.

Her uncle reached into his pocket and pulled out the papers. "But my niece is mad."

The constable turned his gaze to Alden. "Is yer wife mad, sir?" he asked. "Do ye want her put away?"

Alden shook his head, his voice resolute. "My wife has never been, nor ever will be, mad."

"That is good enough for me," the constable said. "I recommend ye get a warrant from the sheriff tae have the marriage officially registered by the local registrar. Guid day."

Once the constable departed from the room, Alden met Lord Inglewood's gaze. "You are no longer welcome here, my lord. Pack your trunks at once and leave us."

"I am still Elinor's uncle," he declared, his voice rising in defiance.

Elinor released Alden's hand and approached her uncle. "Why, Uncle?" she asked. "Why would you go to such great lengths for me to marry a decrepit man?"

Her uncle pursed his lips, his expression sour. "I don't answer to you."

"No, but I do believe you owe me an explanation," Elinor said. "My father would have been so disappointed in you."

His eyes flashed with anger. "I am tired of hearing what a saint your father was. You would think he walked on water. I am not him! I am my own man!" he shouted. "And I needed your dowry to keep the estate afloat. The duke agreed to return the dowry to me if you married him."

"That is despicable," Aunt Cecilia muttered under her breath.

In a calm, collected voice, Elinor said, "I agree with my husband. You are no longer welcome here."

"Elinor—" her uncle started.

She put her hand up, cutting him off. "You can save your breath. Nothing you say will change my mind."

Her uncle narrowed his eyes at Alden, seething. "This is all your fault! You ruined everything. I should challenge you to a duel."

Alden took a step forward, his expression unyielding. "Name the time and place—"

Elinor interjected, "Absolutely not! No one is going to fight a duel. That is the end of the discussion."

Her uncle harrumphed. "I see who wears the pants in your marriage," he muttered.

"It is time for you to go, Uncle," Elinor said. Her voice brooked no argument.

"Fine," her uncle said, waggling his finger at her. "But mark my words, you will regret marrying Mr. Dandridge."

Elinor moved to stand by Alden. "I don't think I will."

Her uncle performed an exaggerated bow before departing from the drawing room, leaving Elinor with her husband.

Her husband.

What had she been thinking?

Chapter Fourteen

Alden couldn't quite believe what had just happened. He had a wife now. And it was Elinor. He had gotten precisely what he had wanted. Now he would inherit the horse farm. But by the look on Elinor's face, it was evident that she was far from pleased. Not that he blamed her. She had been adamant about only marrying for love, and now she found herself bound to him in a marriage of necessity. He hoped she would eventually see it as the better option compared to an asylum.

Mrs. Hardy's voice broke through the silence. "Well, that was rather exciting," she said, turning to Alden. "Thank you for what you did for Elinor. You saved her from Lord Inglewood."

Elinor nodded, albeit reluctantly. "Yes, thank you."

Glancing between them, Mrs. Hardy said, "I do believe that much needs to be said between you two. Why don't I give you a moment?"

"I think that would be for the best," Alden responded, his eyes lingering on Elinor. He would give anything to know what she was thinking at this precise moment.

Mrs. Hardy offered her niece an encouraging smile before she left the room, closing the door softly behind her.

Alden wanted to reach out to touch Elinor, to comfort her, but he didn't think she was ready for that. He just needed to be patient with her. He decided to settle on a safe question. "How are you faring?"

Elinor sighed. "I don't know," she replied. "I don't feel any different now that I am married, but everything has changed."

"That it has," he agreed.

In a hesitant voice, Elinor asked, "Why did you do it?"

He took a step closer to her, unable to resist the urge to be near her. "I couldn't stand by and let your uncle take you to an asylum."

"I can't believe he would do something so underhanded," Elinor said, shaking her head in disbelief.

"Neither could I."

Elinor lowered her gaze to the lapels of his jacket. "Well, you got precisely what you wanted. You will inherit the horse farm."

"This is not how I wanted to go about it," Alden said, his tone earnest. "You must know that."

"I do," she murmured.

Alden placed his finger under her chin and lifted her head until their eyes met. "I promise that I will be a good husband to you."

Elinor's eyes searched his, and he hoped she could see the sincerity in his promise. "I believe you."

"Will you not promise to be a good wife to me?" he teased.

"I will, assuming you do not expect me to obey you," Elinor said. "I do not respond well to being ordered about."

His lips quirked into a small smile. "I do know that about you."

She bit her lower lip, drawing his attention to her perfectly formed lips. "What of marital relations?"

"What of them?" he asked, his voice gentle.

In a hesitant voice, she inquired, "Am I expected to perform them?"

Alden knew there was a time and place to joke with his wife and this was not the time to do so. "Not if you are not willing," he replied. "If you would prefer, this could be a marriage of convenience."

"Do you not require an heir?" Elinor asked.

"I would like one, but not until you are comfortable in doing so," Alden responded. "I won't force you to do anything."

The tension in Elinor's shoulders eased just a fraction. "That is most kind of you."

"Nothing has changed between us," Alden said, dropping his finger from her chin. "We are still friends."

Elinor's eyes grew wide. "Everything has changed. We are married, and you are going to sell the horse farm."

"About that," Alden started, "I was thinking about keeping the horse farm, at least since it is profitable."

A bright smile spread across Elinor's face, her eyes sparkling with joy. "Are you in earnest?"

"I am," Alden confirmed with a nod.

Elinor threw her arms around Alden, pulling him into a tight embrace. He could feel the warmth of gratitude and it filled him with a deep sense of satisfaction. "Thank you. That means more to me than you will ever know."

Alden wrapped his arms around her, savoring the closeness. "I do hope you don't mind continuing to run the horse farm."

"I would prefer it, actually," Elinor declared.

After a moment, Elinor dropped her arms and took a step back. Alden immediately missed the lack of contact.

"With my dowry, you could buy land in England," Elinor suggested.

Alden had completely forgotten about her dowry in the chaos of the moment. "May I ask how much your dowry is?"

"Twenty thousand pounds," she replied.

He stared at Elinor, stunned. "Twenty thousand pounds?" he repeated, his voice tinged with disbelief.

Elinor eyed him with amusement. "I do hope that is sufficient."

"Sufficient?" he asked, shaking his head in amazement. "You are an heiress. How did I not know this?"

"You never asked," Elinor retorted with a shrug.

Alden cocked his head. "What other secrets are you keeping from me?" he asked, half-joking, but with a hint of genuine curiosity.

Elinor stiffened slightly, her playful demeanor fading. "Nothing," she said, her tone more guarded.

He found himself curious by her response, but he didn't want to press her now. He hoped that, in time, she would trust him enough to confide in him.

Bringing a hand to her stomach, Elinor asked, "Would you mind if we returned to the dining room for the feast. I am rather famished."

"I could always eat," Alden responded, offering his arm. "Would you be opposed if I collected my things and moved into the manor now that we are married?"

Elinor placed her hand on his arm as she said, "I shall have the guest bedchamber readied for you."

"Unless you wish to share a bedchamber?" he asked with a flirtatious wink, unable to resist teasing her.

She withdrew her hand and took a step back, her cheeks flushing. "I... uh..." she stammered.

"I am teasing you, Elinor," he rushed out, taking pity on her discomfort. "I'm sorry. It was too soon to do such a thing."

"No, it is all right," Elinor assured him.

Alden grinned, feeling a sense of relief. "This is new to both of us. I have never had a wife before."

Elinor stepped forward and took his arm again, her touch sending a shiver down his spine. "I never thought I would have an irregular marriage in Scotland."

"It will be a good story to share with our children when they are older," Alden said.

"Children?" Elinor asked. "You want more than one?"

Alden started leading Elinor out of the drawing room. "I know we haven't discussed it, but I would like a big family, assuming that is something you would like."

Elinor grew quiet, and Alden feared that he had upset her. He glanced at her, searching for any sign of distress. Finally, after a long moment, she said, "I always wanted a large family. It was quite lonely being an only child."

"Well, look at that, we agreed on something," Alden joked, trying to lighten the mood. "Although, I could have done without my brother."

"You don't mean that," Elinor said softly, her eyes filled with empathy.

Alden opened the door of the drawing room as he responded, "Alexander is the bane of my existence. He criticizes everything I do and say."

"That sounds awful," Elinor murmured.

"It is," Alden agreed, his voice heavy from the weight of past grievances. "But that's a story for another time. For now, let us enjoy the feast and our new beginning."

As Alden led Elinor to the dining room, he could sense her apprehension. Her steps were hesitant, her grip on his arm slightly tense. Truth be told, he was scared, too. This marriage, though hastily arranged, was something he had wanted. But Elinor had not wanted this. She had been adamant about marrying for love, not out of necessity. Which meant he had a challenging task ahead of him- he would need to woo his wife.

Dressed in a white wrapper, Elinor sat on the settee in her

bedchamber, her eyes fixed on the crackling fire. She was a wife now. Everything had changed, yet she felt exactly the same. How was that even possible?

She didn't regret marrying Alden, but she wished it had been under different circumstances. She cared for him, more than she dared admit, but she was scared. Alden was a perfect gentleman, but she wanted more than just a marriage of convenience- she wanted love. The thought of spending her life pining after a husband who might never love her back filled her with dread.

A soft knock came at the door, interrupting her thoughts. The door creaked open, revealing her aunt with a knowing smile. "I see that I was correct in my assumption that you would still be awake."

"Of course I am awake," Elinor responded, her voice tinged with frustration. "I can't get my mind to stop racing."

Her aunt closed the door and approached her, concern etched on her face. "Anything you wish to share?"

Elinor sighed deeply. "I am married now."

Her aunt's smile grew. "I know," she replied, settling beside her. "I was there when Alden saved you from your uncle."

"He did save me, for which I am most grateful, but I find that I am angry at my uncle for forcing my hand," Elinor shared.

"There is nothing wrong with that, especially since Lord Inglewood is a blackguard," her aunt said firmly.

Elinor clasped her hands in her lap, searching for the right words. But what could she say that would express her internal turmoil? Finally, after a long moment, she settled on, "I am scared."

"You, scared?" her aunt teased lightly. "That doesn't sound like you."

"I don't know how to be a wife," Elinor said, her voice trembling.

The humor left her aunt's expression, replaced with compassion. "When I married John, I felt the same way. I was thrust into a home that I was unfamiliar with, and I was expected to run the household. But I buckled down and I got the job done."

"Surely it couldn't have been that simple," Elinor remarked in disbelief.

Her aunt laughed. "No, it wasn't," she replied. "I made mistakes- loads of them. But there is no shame in asking for help, especially from your husband."

Elinor's gaze turned downcast. "I do not like to ask for help."

Her aunt placed a gentle hand over Elinor's clasped hands. "Trust your husband. You may have started off your marriage differently than you expected, but you decide how the story goes from here."

"But he won't ever love me," Elinor said, her voice barely above a whisper. "He has told me as much."

Her aunt lifted a brow. "Do you love him?"

Elinor brought her gaze up to meet her aunt's. "No, but I could," she admitted softly.

"Give it time, my dear," her aunt counseled. "You never know what your future will hold around Christmastime."

"And if he doesn't come to love me?" Elinor asked.

Her aunt removed her hand and leaned back. "Then I shall play my bagpipes for him until he changes his mind."

"I am serious."

"So am I," her aunt said with a twinkle in her eyes.

Elinor felt her stomach rumble, drawing another laugh from her aunt. "I am famished," she admitted.

Her aunt grinned. "I assumed that would be the case since you didn't eat very much during dinner."

"How could I?" Elinor asked.

"It is quite a simple process," her aunt joked. "You dip your fork into food and bring that said fork up to your lips."

Elinor rose and walked over to the window, staring out into the expansive darkness. "How can you make light of everything right now?"

"You are married, not dead," her aunt said. "And I believe Mr. Dandridge to be an honorable man."

"I cannot believe that Alden has won you over," Elinor remarked.

Rising, her aunt asked, "And why wouldn't he? He saved you from being committed." She approached her and placed a hand on Elinor's shoulder. "Why don't you go eat something from the kitchen? I asked Mrs. Beaton to leave a plate out for you."

Elinor's stomach rumbled again. "I could eat."

Her aunt laughed. "I can always eat. It is a terrible curse, really."

Turning towards her aunt, Elinor said, "Thank you."

"For what, my dear?"

Elinor grew solemn. "For speaking about your husband," she replied. "I know how much it pains you to speak of Uncle John."

Her aunt withdrew her hand, and her eyes grew sad. "I miss John. Every single day. We may have only had a short time together, but what we did have will last forever."

"I hope to love Alden as much as you loved John," Elinor said.

"You will," her aunt replied. "Opening your heart is scary, but sometimes the only way to protect it is to open it."

Elinor knew her aunt was only trying to help but surely it couldn't be that simple. What if she loved Alden and he never returned that love? The uncertainty gnawed at her, but she knew she had to take one step at a time. For now, she would go eat something.

"I suppose I should eat before it gets too late," Elinor said, trying to push aside her worries.

Her aunt glanced out the darkened window. "I think that

ship has sailed since it is almost midnight," she joked. "But come, I will walk you down to the kitchen."

"There is no need. I can go on my own," Elinor insisted, noticing the yawn that had just escaped her aunt's lips.

"I am rather tired," her aunt admitted.

"Then you should go to bed," Elinor encouraged gently.

"Very well," her aunt said, walking over to the door. She stopped and turned back, her face softening with a look of regret. "I'm sorry your uncle ruined Christmas for you."

As Elinor approached her, she responded, "I will admit that it made for a very interesting Christmas this year."

"Interesting?" her aunt asked, opening the door. "That is not the word I would have used."

Elinor followed her aunt into the darkened corridor and said, "Goodnight, Aunt Cecilia."

"Goodnight, my dearest," her aunt said before she disappeared into her own bedchamber, leaving Elinor alone with her thoughts.

Elinor made her way to the kitchen, her steps echoing softly in the quiet manor. She carefully descended the servants' stairs, the cool stone underfoot adding to her awareness of the late hour.

As she reached the kitchen, she realized she was not alone. A shadowed figure was moving about, making an absurd amount of noise. Her heart skipped a beat until the moonlight streaming through the windows revealed Alden's face. Relief washed over her at his presence.

"Alden," she said softly.

He turned towards her, surprise evident on his face. "Elinor? What are you doing awake?"

She moved closer, standing beside him. "I could ask you the same thing."

He gave her a sheepish grin. "I'm afraid I am rather famished, and I was looking for something to eat."

"Did you check the table?" she asked, pointing to the plate with a white linen napkin draped over it.

Alden shook his head, a smile tugging at his lips. "That would have been far too simple."

"Would you care to join me in seeing what Mrs. Beaton left us to eat?" Elinor asked.

He gestured towards the table with a flourish. "After you," he replied.

Elinor took a seat, waiting until Alden settled beside her before reaching for the napkin. With an exaggerated motion, she pulled it off, revealing a modest spread of bread, cheese and meat.

"Ladies first," he said.

She reached for a piece of bread and began to eat. After a long moment of comfortable silence, she decided to speak up. "Will you tell me about yourself?"

Alden plopped a piece of cheese into his mouth, chewing thoughtfully. "What would you like to know?"

"I suppose we should start from the beginning," Elinor replied. "What were you like as a child?"

"I was the handsomest of children," Alden said with a grin.

Elinor laughed. "Of course you were," she responded. "But I am more curious as to what you were like growing up."

Alden leaned back in his chair, his expression thoughtful. "Well, I was always getting into trouble. My brother and I had quite the rivalry, always trying to outdo each other. I suppose it made me who I am today."

"Tell me more. What kind of trouble did you get into?"

He chuckled. "Oh, where to start? There was a time we tried to build a raft to sail down the river. It fell apart almost immediately, and we ended up soaked and covered in mud. Mother was furious."

Elinor smiled, imagining a younger Alden covered in mud. "That sounds like quite the adventure."

"It was," Alden agreed. "But enough about me. I want to learn more about you."

"I am not that interesting," Elinor attempted.

Alden leaned forward in his seat, his gaze unwavering. "I disagree," he said. "I find you to be utterly fascinating."

The intensity of Alden's gaze made a blush form on Elinor's cheeks. She struggled to keep her voice steady, feeling the warmth of his presence. "You are kind."

"It is merely the truth, Elinor," Alden said, moving closer. "I wouldn't have married you otherwise."

Alden was so close now that she could catch the faint, tantalizing scent of orange wafting from his person. It was intoxicating. She wanted to close the distance between them, to give in to the urge to kiss him. But she held herself back. If she kissed him now, there would be no going back, and she wasn't ready to risk her heart just yet.

Chapter Fifteen

Alden knew he needed to move slowly with Elinor, and all he had was time now that she was his wife. As much as he wanted to kiss her, he knew that Elinor wasn't ready.

He leaned back in his chair and picked up a piece of cheese off the plate. "Now, tell me more about yourself and do not leave out any details."

"That could take all night."

"Do you have anywhere else you need to be?" Alden asked, his eyes sparkling with a playful challenge.

Elinor smiled. "My bed, considering I enjoy sleeping."

Alden returned her smile. "All right, we will just converse until we finish the food. Then you can go to bed and sleep."

Glancing down at the plate, Elinor said, "I believe I already told you that I had a wonderful childhood."

"You did, and you were rather mischievous."

"I was," Elinor said, her eyes lighting up. "I loved wearing trousers and riding my horse bareback, but at some point, everyone has to grow up."

"Well, I do not take issue if you want to wear trousers to go riding," Alden said, reaching for a piece of bread.

Elinor's brow shot up. "You don't?"

He held his hands out wide. "I don't know why you sound so surprised. We are on the outskirts of the village, and I don't think anyone would give it much heed."

"Thank you," Elinor said. "That means a great deal to me."

Alden held her gaze, his expression earnest. "I want you to be happy, Elinor. I hope you know that."

Elinor nodded. "I do."

"Good, because maybe I will wear a kilt and go riding a horse," Alden quipped.

She laughed, just as he had intended. "That would be quite a sight to see," she said. "I don't think the grooms could handle that."

Alden chuckled. "I don't think *I* could handle that."

"My father always encouraged me to be who I wanted to be. He said that life was too short to be someone you weren't meant to be," Elinor shared.

"That is some good advice."

Elinor offered him a weak smile. "My father would have liked you."

"From the way you speak of your father, I have no doubt that I would have liked him as well," he said. "Same with your mother."

"No, my mother would not have liked you, at least at first," Elinor remarked.

Alden brought a hand to his chest, feigning outrage. "And why is that?"

Elinor gave him a knowing look. "You were far too cocky when I first met you."

"That is because I had to make a good first impression on you," Alden said. "I take it that I failed."

"Only a little," Elinor said with a grin.

"If I made such a poor impression, why did you agree to help me?" Alden inquired, his curiosity piqued.

The humor left Elinor's face and her eyes grew guarded. "That was different."

Alden's brow furrowed, sensing the shift in her mood. "Did I say something wrong?"

"No…" Elinor said, pushing back the plate. "It is late, and I am growing tired."

"Don't go," Alden said, not quite ready for her to leave. "Not yet. We can talk about anything that you would like to."

Elinor considered him for a long moment before asking, "Would you have truly married Miss Cowen?"

Alden huffed. "Heavens, no!" he replied. "I was just trying to make you jealous."

"You were?"

Finding himself curious, he asked, "Did it work?"

Elinor lowered her gaze before admitting, "If I were to be honest, I was a little jealous."

Alden felt elated by what Elinor had just admitted. Perhaps she did care for him, just as he did for her. "How could you ever think I would marry Miss Cowen?"

"You wanted the horse farm," Elinor said with a slight shrug.

"I did, but I was just biding my time until I could convince you to marry me," Alden admitted.

Elinor brought her gaze up, her eyes searching his. "What if I had never agreed to marry you?"

"That is impossible," Alden said with a boyish grin. "I can be quite charming when I want to be."

"I'm afraid I haven't seen it," Elinor retorted playfully.

Alden shook his head, smiling at her teasing. "You do know how to keep a man humble."

"What of Mrs. MacBain or Miss Fraser? Did you fancy either of them?" Elinor asked.

"No," he replied. "From the moment I set eyes on you, I have only been interested in pursuing you. I just couldn't let on what I was doing."

Elinor eyed him curiously. "Why me?"

Alden decided it would be best to tell her the truth and be done with it. "At first, I was beguiled by your beauty, but over time, I realized that your beauty wasn't just skin deep. It went deeper, down to your very soul."

"I don't know if that is true," Elinor said, shifting in her seat.

"No, it is," Alden insisted. "I have known many beautiful women over the years, and none of them could hold a candle to you. You must know how enchanting you are."

Elinor frowned. "I want to be more than a pretty face."

Alden leaned forward. "You are," he rushed to assure her. "You are running a profitable horse farm. That is quite the feat."

"For a woman?" Elinor challenged, arching an eyebrow.

He knew he needed to proceed cautiously. "No, it is quite a feat for anyone- male or female. I do not think I could have done as well as you have, which is why I want you to keep running it."

Elinor winced. "I'm sorry I am so defensive. I am used to being told what I can't do, and not what I can do."

"That ends now since we are married," Alden insisted. "Everything we do, we will do so together."

"That sounds nice," Elinor said softly.

Alden moved his chair closer to Elinor. "I mean it," he replied earnestly. "I want to make this marriage work."

Elinor bit her lower lip, a sure sign she was upset. "Do you think you could ever come to love me?"

He sighed. "I told you that love in a relationship only complicates things," he started, "but that doesn't mean I don't care for you. I do."

"I understand," Elinor said, lowering her gaze.

"I know you want love, but what we have is better," Alden asserted gently. "We get along nicely, and we have genuine affection for one another."

Elinor's eyes grew sad. "I should be happy, but I want more."

Alden reached for her hand and gently held it. "I promise that I will always care for you, and I will be faithful to you. Is that not enough?"

"I suppose it will have to be," she murmured.

"Elinor... I am sorry," Alden said, his voice thick with regret. "I hope I can be enough for you."

Elinor glanced down at their joined hands, but not before he saw the mixture of emotions playing across her face. She wanted more than what he could offer her, and quite frankly, she deserved more. But this was all he could give her... for now.

She slipped her hand out from his. "I should go. It is late."

"May I walk you up to your bedchamber?" he asked, hoping to prolong their time together.

With a slight bob of her head, she replied, "I would like that."

He rose and offered his hand to assist her in rising. Once she stood, she removed her hand and clasped them in front of her.

They started making their way up the servants' stairs and through the manor. Alden was about to break the silence when he saw a house spider scuttle across the hall.

Alden froze and put his hand out to stop Elinor.

"What is wrong?" she asked, her voice laced with concern.

He pointed towards the direction of where he last saw the house spider. "I just saw a spider," he revealed, his voice a bit shaky.

"Where is it?" Elinor asked, her eyes roaming over the hall.

"I don't know where it went," Alden replied, his eyes darting around nervously. "But it is here somewhere."

Elinor turned to face him, her expression softening. "What shall we do?"

"I propose we don't move until we are sure it is gone and won't attack us," Alden said.

"House spiders do not attack people. That is the only thing I am sure of," she assured him. "We could trap it and release it outside."

Alden's mouth dropped in astonishment. "You want to seek out the house spider. Are you mad?"

"At least I am the only one coming up with ideas," she replied, a hint of amusement in her voice. "Besides, it is not as if we can stand here all night."

"You are right," Alden said, offering his arm. "I shall protect you."

Elinor looked amused. "You?"

"That is the job of any good husband," Alden responded, puffing out his chest. He hoped that he sounded more confident than he felt.

She patted his arm. "I think it is safe to proceed. I don't see the house spider."

As they continued to head down the corridor, Alden kept his alert gaze out for the house spider. He relaxed slightly when they reached the grand stairs.

Finally, they arrived at her bedchamber door. Alden turned to her, his heart heavy with unspoken words. "Goodnight, Elinor," he said.

"Goodnight, Alden," she replied, her voice holding an emotion he couldn't quite place.

Unexpectedly, Elinor went to her tiptoes and pressed her lips to his. He was so surprised that he didn't even have time to react. The next moment, she disappeared into her room.

Alden stood there, stunned. Elinor had kissed him, and everything changed. He found he wasn't satisfied with that one kiss. He wanted more. But did Elinor feel the same?

One thing was for certain, that kiss sparked something deep within him, making him realize that he loved his wife.

Elinor lay in bed, staring up at the canopy, her thoughts in turmoil. She had kissed her husband last night. What had she been thinking? He had told her that he couldn't love her, and she responded by kissing him? The kiss had only confirmed what she already knew deep down. That she loved him. What was she going to do? How could she get Alden to love her?

A knock came at the door, interrupting her thoughts. It opened and Sophia stepped into the room, placing a stack of coins onto the dressing table.

Elinor looked at her lady's maid in confusion. "What is that?"

Sophia rubbed her hands together nervously. "It is the money that Lord Inglewood gave to me," she revealed.

Sitting up in bed, Elinor asked, "I beg your pardon?"

"It is my fault that Lord Inglewood knew where you were," Sophia replied, lowering her gaze.

"*What?!*" Elinor asked. "That is how he found me? It was you?"

Sophia nodded, her voice trembling. "My younger sister is a maid in Lord Inglewood's household in London, and I wrote to her," she said. "I wanted to make sure that she was well, but I didn't think she would turn the letter over to Lord Inglewood."

"And he gave you money?"

"I didn't want to accept it, but he left it with Bryon," Sophia revealed, her eyes filling with tears. "I assure you, I didn't mean for this to happen."

Elinor swung her feet over the side of the bed, standing up. "I believe you," she replied. There was no reason not to believe Sophia, considering she had always been loyal to her.

Sophia looked up, tears streaming down her cheeks. "You

have been so kind to me, and I would never want to betray your trust."

"There is only one solution, then," Elinor said.

Wiping at her cheeks, Sophia asked, "I'm dismissed?"

Elinor shook her head. "No. You ask your sister to come work here," she suggested. "You could use the coins to pay for her travel."

Sophia's eyes grew wide. "You mean that?"

"I hadn't realized that your sister worked for Lord Inglewood or else I would have suggested it earlier," Elinor responded.

"I didn't wish to burden you."

Elinor approached Sophia, placing a comforting hand on her shoulder. "From now on, please tell me the truth, whether or not you think it might burden me."

Sophia smiled through the tears. "I promise."

"Good," Elinor said, hesitating for a moment. "Now that is resolved, I need your help. I kissed Alden last night."

"You did?" Sophia asked, her eyes widening with curiosity.

"Yes, and now I am conflicted," Elinor confessed. "Last night, he told me he could never love me."

Sophia looked at her oddly. "So you kissed him?"

Elinor tossed her hands up in the air in exasperation. "Not right away," she said. "He walked me to the door and was looking at me in such a fashion that I couldn't resist."

"This is a good thing," Sophia attempted to reassure her.

"How?"

Sophia shrugged. "He is your husband, and you clearly have some affection for him."

"I do, but…" She let out a loud groan of frustration. "What was I thinking? I was too brazen."

"That is not brazen, my lady," Sophia assured her. "I could tell you stories about the ladies that used to visit Lord Inglewood."

"Please don't," Elinor said.

Sophia laughed. "I promise, I won't," she said, walking over to the wardrobe. "Let's get you dressed so you can shower your husband with more kisses."

Elinor frowned in mock irritation. "I should have dismissed you," she joked.

"It is too late now," Sophia said, retrieving a pale blue gown. "I think this dress will do quite nicely for today."

"It is far too fancy," Elinor remarked.

Sophia held it up, examining it critically. "Not if we want Mr. Dandridge to fall in love with you."

Elinor slumped into the chair by the dressing table. "Are you even listening to me?"

"I am," Sophia said, her tone serious now. "I am rather convinced that Mr. Dandridge cares for you just as much as you care for him."

"He does care for me, he admitted as much, but that is a far cry from love," Elinor said.

"If that is the case, it makes me wonder why you care so much," Sophia remarked. "Do you love him?"

Elinor's mouth dropped open, feigning outrage. "No."

Sophia gave her a pointed look. "The truth, please."

With a sigh, Elinor confessed, "Yes."

"Then we need to get your husband to fall in love with you," Sophia declared with determination.

"I don't think a gown is going to help with that," Elinor said doubtfully.

Sophia laid the gown onto the bed before approaching the dressing table. She removed Elinor's cap from her head and picked up the brush. "It couldn't hurt. Besides, you are going to take advantage of your incomparable beauty."

"Sophia..."

Her lady's maid spoke over her. "You should laugh at everything he says, as if he were the world's most clever man," she said.

Elinor rolled her eyes. "That sounds nothing like me."

"You are right," Sophia conceded, placing down the brush. "I propose a new plan. You are going to wear trousers in front of him. That will show off your curves."

"No, I am going to use my mind to win him over," Elinor asserted.

"That could take much longer," Sophia said as she twisted Elinor's hair in a chignon. "I like my plan better."

Once Sophia had pinned up her hair, Elinor shifted in her seat to face her lady's maid. "I need to tell him the truth."

Sophia looked bemused. "About what?"

With a sheepish look, Elinor replied, "How I wasn't truly trying to help him secure a wife because I wanted to inherit the horse farm."

"I don't think that is a wise idea."

"Regardless, I can't start this marriage with secrets," Elinor said firmly. "It is the right thing to do."

Sophia didn't look convinced. "Is it?"

"Yes," Elinor replied, her voice resolute.

"Why don't we work on getting him to fall in love with you first?" Sophia pressed. "Then he might not care when you tell him the truth."

Elinor rose from her seat. "I have to do it today."

Sophia glanced around the room. "I quite liked this place. It is a shame that your husband will kick us out of here."

"Do not be so dramatic," Elinor said.

The door opened and Aunt Cecilia stepped into the room. "Now that you are married, do you want a tray to be brought to your room?"

"No, I will eat breakfast with Alden," Elinor responded.

Her aunt beamed. "I was hoping you would say that. I was just informed by Bryon that Mr. Dandridge is in the dining room."

"Wonderful," Elinor said. "This is the perfect time to tell him the truth."

"The truth?" her aunt repeated.

"Yes, about how I was set to inherit the horse farm if he didn't marry," Elinor replied.

Her aunt exchanged a worried look with Sophia. "Are you sure you want to do that now?" she asked. "I am not saying you shouldn't tell him, but surely there is a better time to do so."

Elinor walked over to the bed and picked up the dress. "This is something I need to do."

"All right," her aunt said. "I support your decision."

"Thank you," Elinor responded.

Sophia approached her and helped her dress. Elinor smoothed down her gown and said, "Wish me luck."

Her aunt spoke up. "Start the conversation by complimenting him," she suggested. "Men love to be flattered."

With an approving nod, Sophia replied, "Mrs. Hardy is right, and be sure to pout. That will bring attention to your lips. It will remind him that you kissed him last night."

"You kissed him?" her aunt asked.

Elinor's lips twitched. "I did," she confirmed.

"Well done," her aunt declared. "I must say that you two have made remarkable progress since yesterday."

Walking over to the door, Elinor said, "Wish me luck."

"You don't need luck, Dear, you just need to keep kissing your husband," her aunt said. "That will distract him from the truth."

"Goodbye, Aunt Cecilia." Elinor departed from her bedchamber and headed down to the main level. She was almost to the dining room when she saw Bryon.

The butler's eyes crinkled around the edges when he saw her. "Good morning, my lady," he said with a tip of his head.

"Good morning," she replied in kind.

"Your husband requested a carriage be brought around front," he informed her. "Apparently, he wants a ride in the countryside with you."

Elinor smiled. "I think that sounds like a splendid idea," she said before she stepped into the dining room.

Alden met her gaze and rose from the head of the table. "Good morning, Wife."

"Good morning, Husband," she responded.

He retrieved a chair, placing it to the right of his. "Come join me for breakfast," he encouraged.

"I would like that very much," Elinor said.

Once they were both situated, a footman stepped forward and placed a plate of food in front of her. She stared at the plate, knowing that much needed to be said between them. And she wasn't quite sure where to start.

Chapter Sixteen

Alden realized he quite liked having Elinor as a wife. For the first time, it seemed as though everything in his life was falling into place. He now owned a thriving horse farm, would soon be collecting Elinor's dowry, and was married to a woman who inspired him to be a better man.

A smile spread across his face as he glanced over at Elinor from the head of the table. "How are you faring this morning?"

Elinor reached for her glass. "I am well," she replied. "I trust that you slept well."

"I did, especially after you kissed me," he said, a teasing note in his voice.

She choked on her drink. "Must you bring that up?" she asked, hastily setting the glass back down on the table.

"Why?" he asked.

"It is not very gentlemanly of you," she chided lightly.

Leaning closer, he said in a low voice, "I am hoping for many more kisses in the future from my beautiful wife."

A blush crept onto Elinor's cheeks, and she dropped her gaze to the table, clearly flustered. "Can we talk about something else, please?"

"All right," he said, taking pity on his wife. "What would you care to discuss?"

Elinor's eyes darted to the footmen standing by the door. "There is something important I need to tell you."

Alden could sense Elinor's discomfort, making him wonder what was so important. He turned to the footmen and ordered, "Leave us."

Once they were alone, Alden gave her an expectant look. "What is wrong?"

"Nothing is wrong," Elinor said, her smile weak and unconvincing. "I just believe we should be honest with one another."

"I agree," he said, leaning back in his chair.

Elinor clasped her hands in her lap, her knuckles white from the pressure. She took a deep breath and said, "Before you arrived, Lady Edith wrote to me and told me of the stipulations of you inheriting the horse farm. But what I didn't tell you was that I would inherit the horse farm if you failed to marry by the Twelfth Night."

Alden wondered how he could love this woman even more than he already did. "And yet you still agreed to help me?" he asked. "You truly are remarkable."

Elinor bit her lower lip. "Actually, I did the opposite."

He furrowed his brow in confusion. "I don't understand."

"While I am acquainted with the three women I introduced you to, we are not dear friends and I knew that you wouldn't be interested in them," Elinor admitted.

Realization hit him, and he felt a mix of hurt and anger. "You tried to sabotage me."

"I did," she replied, her voice breaking.

He stared at her in disbelief. "And sending me to the cottage in the woods?"

Elinor winced. "I wanted you to pack your bags and go home. I thought you wouldn't last the night, considering the state of the cottage."

Alden rose and walked over to the window. Elinor had lied to him. How was he supposed to reconcile with that fact? Finally, after a long moment, he turned to face her. "How could you just lie to me so easily?" he asked, his voice rising. "You led me to believe that you were helping me, but you were just trying to help yourself. What do you have to say for yourself?"

"I wanted the horse farm," Elinor replied honestly.

"And now?" Alden demanded

Rising, Elinor approached him, her eyes pleading. "Everything has changed. We are married—"

He cut her off sharply. "Would you have married me if it wasn't for your uncle forcing your hand?"

"That doesn't matter—"

"Answer the question," he ordered, his tone brooking no argument.

Elinor hesitated. "I don't know."

Alden ran a hand through his hair in frustration. "How can I ever trust you?" he asked. "You tried to take everything from me."

"I'm sorry…" she whispered, her voice breaking.

He scoffed. "You are sorry," Alden said. "No, I am sorry. I can't believe I trusted you so easily. And to think my great-aunt was such a poor judge of character."

Elinor reared back. "I love your Great-aunt Edith."

"Apparently, not enough to do as she asked," Alden retorted.

"Your great-aunt did not ask me to help you," Elinor countered.

Alden lifted his brow skeptically. "That is your defense?" he asked.

Elinor reached out and touched his sleeve. "Alden, I'm sorry. I was wrong—"

He pulled his arm away, watching as her hand fell. "You were wrong, and so was I," he said. "I thought we could have a real marriage between us, but I was just fooling myself. Everything was a lie."

"I love you—" she started to say.

"No!" he exclaimed, the word echoing in the space between them. "Enough of your lies."

Alden saw tears brimming in her eyes, cascading down her cheeks. Her pain was almost palpable, but he forced himself to stay firm.

"I am not lying," Elinor responded. "I didn't want to fall in love with you, but I did. You must believe me."

"Believe you?" he huffed. "I can't even look at you right now."

Another tear escaped her eye and rolled down her cheek. "Alden, please…"

He put up his hand, cutting her off. "You got what you wanted. You can have the horse farm and I will leave Scotland."

Her eyes grew wide. "That is not what I want."

"Well, I don't quite care what you want right now," Alden said coldly before storming out of the dining room.

Alden headed up to his bedchamber, throwing open the door and startling his valet. "What is wrong, sir?" Hastings asked.

"Pack my trunks," he ordered. "We are leaving at once."

Hastings remained rooted in his spot. "May I ask what happened?"

"No, you may not," he snapped. "Just for once, do as you are told."

As his valet went about packing up his clothes, Alden walked over to the window and stared out over the fields. He didn't want a marriage of convenience with Elinor, but that is what it was shaping up to be. He would go his way and she would go hers. He had once told Elinor that he valued honesty above all else, and he meant it.

How could she have just lied to his face so easily, especially with everything that they had gone through? He had trusted her, but she had been plotting for him to fail this whole time.

The door was abruptly opened, and Mrs. Hardy stepped into the room with a stern look on her face. "We need to talk, young man."

"I have nothing to say to you," Alden said, turning to face her.

Mrs. Hardy gave his valet a pointed look. "Leave us."

"He doesn't answer to you—" Alden started, but his valet swiftly departed from the room, closing the door behind him.

She crossed her arms over her chest. "Why is my niece crying in the dining room?" she demanded.

"This is none of your business," he said.

"You made it my business when you upset my niece," Mrs. Hardy said. "I suspect this has to do with her lying to you."

Alden's eyes narrowed. "You knew?"

She tossed her hands in the air, exasperated. "Of course I knew. I even encouraged her to do so."

"Why would you do that?"

She approached him, coming to a stop a short distance away. "My niece is many things, but she is stubborn, almost to a fault. She had to keep busy in order to overlook what was right in front of her."

"Which was?"

She pointed directly at him. "Falling in love with you."

Alden looked heavenward. "Not this again," he muttered. "How do I know she isn't lying just to keep what she has?"

"What does she have to gain by lying now?" Mrs. Hardy asked.

"Regardless, I have made my decision," Alden stated firmly. "I am leaving Scotland and Elinor will continue to run the horse farm. She wins. She got precisely what she wanted."

Mrs. Hardy lowered her finger, her expression softening with compassion. "That is not what she wants, at least not anymore," she insisted. "I know you are scared, but you must not let the lessons, the experiences of your past, harden your heart. You deserve a new beginning with Elinor."

He looked at Mrs. Hardy incredulously. "How can I even trust Elinor again?" he asked.

"She could have kept this from you, but she decided to tell you the truth. What does that say about her?" Mrs. Hardy asked.

"My mother would lie to my father…" Alden began

Mrs. Hardy stepped closer to him, her voice gentle but firm. "Elinor is not your mother, and you are not your father. You two love one another."

"I never said I loved Elinor," Alden stated.

"You didn't have to," Mrs. Hardy said. "I can see it in your face, in your eyes, and hear it in your voice. You love Elinor."

Alden turned away from Mrs. Hardy, finding himself conflicted. "So what if I do?" he asked. "Am I supposed to just forgive her and move on?"

"Yes," she replied.

"It is not that simple," Alden declared. He wanted to believe Elinor, but the wound was too fresh, the betrayal too deep. How could he just move past this?

Mrs. Hardy shook her head, her voice filled with emotion. "I have loved one man in my life, and I would do anything to spend one more day with him," she said, her words cracking with emotion. "Love doesn't come around very often. My question is: what do you intend to do about it?"

Alden watched as Mrs. Hardy spun around on her heel and walked over to the door. She placed her hand on the handle and stopped. "In your heart, you know what the right thing to do is," she advised.

Once Mrs. Hardy departed from the room, his valet stepped back in with questions in his eyes. "Sir?" he asked.

Alden had a choice to make. He could do what he always did and leave, or he could stay and fight for what truly mattered- Elinor. The woman that he loved and would always love.

Botheration.

He couldn't leave Elinor, not now. If he did, he knew he would always regret it. She had quickly become his everything, and no one else could surpass her in his heart, now and always.

Glancing at the open trunks, Alden asked, "Is love worth the risk?"

His valet gave him an understanding look. "Only if you've found the right woman."

Alden closed his eyes, a wave of realization washing over him. "I have," he replied. And that was the truth. No one would ever compare to Elinor. She was his, and he was hers.

"Then my advice is to hold on to her and don't let her go," Hastings counseled. "Life is much better when you have the woman you love by your side."

Determined, Alden walked over to the door. "You might as well unpack. If I have my way, I won't ever be leaving. But I did make a muck of things."

Hastings smiled. "Go to her, sir."

Elinor tightened the cloak around her as she stepped into the stables. She needed to be alone with her thoughts. How had everything gone so terribly wrong? It was all her fault, and she knew it. She should never have tried to deceive Alden. But if she hadn't, would she have still been married to him?

As she walked down the aisle, Calen greeted her with a tip of his head while brushing down one of the horses in a stall. "Guid mornin', my lady," he greeted.

"Good morning," she responded, stopping at the stall. "How is everything?"

Calen paused with the brushing. "Everythin's gaein' weel. The horses have missed ye the past few days."

"I'm afraid I have been rather preoccupied," Elinor admitted.

"Would ye care tae dae some ridin'?"

Elinor shook her head. "I am just here to visit with the horses."

"Then I willnae bother ye," he said as he started to resume brushing down the horse.

She continued down the aisle until she saw Skye. The horse nickered when she saw her, and Elinor laughed. "Hello, Skye," she greeted. "Would you care for an apple?"

Reaching down, she retrieved an apple from the bucket and extended it towards Skye. The horse quickly gobbled it up, causing her to smile.

She tried to convince herself that she didn't need Alden. She had her horses, the manor, and her aunt. She had every-thing she needed. But even she couldn't fathom that lie. She wanted Alden. No, she *needed* Alden. He had changed her, and for the better. She didn't quite feel so lonely anymore now that he was in her life. And she had ruined that.

The worst part was that she didn't regret telling him the truth. She didn't want to start out their marriage with lies. She wanted honesty between them. However, she didn't think he would truly leave her. Perhaps he didn't care for her enough to stay and fight for her.

Elinor's eyes filled with tears and she blinked them back. It would do no good if she cried. It was her fault. She just needed to move on and learn to live without Alden.

Alden's voice came from the doorway. "Elinor," he said gently.

She closed her eyes. What now? Was he here to yell at her some more?

"Elinor," he repeated as he walked closer, his boots grinding on the straw lining the floor of the stables.

She turned to face him and hastily wiped at the tears that were threatening to fall from her eyes. "Alden," she responded.

Alden cast his eyes at the stall where Calen was.

Calen cleared his throat. "Pardon me, sir," he said. "I was just aboot tae take a break, as are the other grooms."

Neither of them spoke as the grooms departed from the stables, leaving them alone. Elinor eyed Alden curiously, wondering what he was doing here. She thought he was leaving. But she was glad that he was here... with her.

Alden remained rooted in his spot, his expression unreadable. "You lied to me."

Elinor nodded. "I did, and I am terribly sorry."

"You tried to steal my inheritance," Alden said.

With a slight wince, she admitted, "Yes, I did, and I was wrong to do so. I know that now." Was he just here to torture her?

Alden took a step towards her, his eyes not wavering from hers. "Thank you for saying so, but it changes nothing between us."

Her heart dropped. "I understand," she said, placing her hand on Skye's neck to steady herself. "I thought you were leaving."

"I was, but I had a riveting conversation with your aunt," he informed her. "She encouraged me to stay. She told me that you loved me."

Elinor sighed deeply. "I do, and that will never change." There. That was the truth. She knew in her heart that she would always love him.

"Then we have a problem," Alden said, his tone softening.

She dropped her hand from Skye, confusion etching her features. "We do?"

Alden nodded. "I say that nothing has changed between us, because it is true," he said. "I have fallen in love with you. Desperately so."

Her eyes widened in surprise. "You love me?" she asked.

In a few purposeful strides, he closed the distance between them. "I wanted to leave, but I couldn't. I love you, Elinor."

"But I thought you said that love complicates marriages?"

"It does, but I am willing to take that chance. With you," he said, his voice filled with resolve. "Assuming you feel the same."

Elinor stared up at him in disbelief, her heart pounding. "Does this mean you forgive me for lying to you?"

"It does, assuming we will always be honest with one another from here on out," Alden replied.

"I can agree to that."

Alden stepped closer, causing her to tilt her head to look up at him. "Then I propose we change our agreement," he said. "I want a real marriage, one where I can kiss you whenever I want."

Elinor felt excitement build up inside of her. "I want that, as well."

"Then there is only one thing we need to do," Alden responded, leaning in towards her. "We must kiss on it."

"I am not opposed to that—"

She had barely uttered her words when Alden's lips met hers. His kiss was both gentle and fierce, a blend of vulnerability and strength. He wrapped his arms around her, pulling her in close, and she surrendered to his touch. How she loved this man. He made her feel safe, loved, and as their lips touched, she tasted forever.

Alden broke the kiss but remained close, his warm breath on her skin. "You don't know how long I have waited to kiss you like that."

"Why stop now?" she asked with a coy smile.

He chuckled. "I think the grooms need to get back to work."

"You are probably right," Elinor said. "Thank you for staying with me."

Alden returned her smile. "I don't think I was capable of leaving you."

"I love you," she whispered, her voice trembling with emotion.

"I know, and I love you with my whole heart," Alden said. "Although, I will now have the unfortunate task of introducing you to my family."

Elinor bobbed her head. "I would like to meet them."

"No, trust me, you don't," he teased. "They will no doubt love you, just as I do, but I do not seek out their approval. I made my choice, and I know it is the right one."

"I was so scared that I lost you forever," she admitted softly, her voice barely above a whisper.

Alden brought his hand up and cupped her right cheek. "I was angry, but I was also scared. I am not scared anymore."

Elinor felt tears pricking in the back of her eyes. "I am not scared either."

"Good, because we have a lifetime together," Alden said, taking a step back and dropping his hand. "And our new beginning starts now."

As Alden reached for her hand, a bright smile spread across her face. She was happy- far happier than she had ever been. She had a marriage that she had always dreamed of. One that would be filled with love.

This may have started as a ruse, but it ended with a prize that she hadn't anticipated: Alden. For he was far better than any horse farm.

Epilogue

Two weeks later...

Alden stood in front of Skye's stall and offered her an apple. The horse eyed him cautiously, her ears flicking back and forth, before finally accepting the proffered treat with a gentle nudge.

He brought his hand up and rubbed the horse's neck, feeling the softness of her coat beneath his fingers. "Why don't you like me, Skye?" he asked.

Calen, who was sweeping the stables, chuckled as he leaned on his broom. "Aye, that's a tricky question, seeing as Skye has only really taken tae Lady Elinor."

Alden dropped his hand and sighed. "Well, I don't blame Skye. After all, I am rather taken by my wife, as well," he said with a hint of amusement. "But it would be nice if Skye didn't try to nip at me when we all go on a ride together."

"Give it time," Calen encouraged, offering him a reassuring smile.

Alden took a step back. "All the other horses seem to like me, especially when I give them apples."

Elinor's voice came from the doorway of the stables. "You poor man," she teased. "Why are you insistent that everyone has to like you?"

"Not everyone, just Skye," Alden said with a smile, turning to face his wife.

Elinor approached him, her black cloak trailing along the floor of the stables, the soft rustle of fabric mingling with the quiet sounds of the horses. "Isn't it enough that I like you?" she asked, her eyes twinkling with mischief.

"You just like me?" he repeated, raising an eyebrow.

She grinned, coming to a stop in front of him. "Perhaps I like you a little more than that." She went on her tiptoes and pressed her lips against his. "Good morning."

"Good morning," he repeated, wrapping his arms around her.

Calen leaned the broom against the wall and cleared his throat. "I'll give ye two a moment. I have work tae dea on the west fence anyways."

Once the groom was gone, Alden asked, "Now, where were we?"

"I think you were going to tell me that you are madly in love with me," Elinor said with a playful smirk. "And how you cannot live without me."

Alden chuckled. "Both are true."

"I know. That is why I said them," Elinor retorted.

Remaining close, Alden said, "I received word from my mother this morning. My family intends to visit us within a fortnight."

"Wonderful," Elinor responded, her eyes lighting up.

Alden shook his head with a wry smile. "I daresay you will change your mind once you meet them."

Elinor gave him an amused look. "I will love them, just as I love you."

"You love me now?" Alden teased. "I thought you only 'liked' me a moment ago."

She laughed, the sound warming his heart. "I love you more than the horse farm."

"That is quite a lot," Alden responded.

"I know, which is why you should be nice to me," Elinor said.

Alden leaned closer and kissed her, a slow and gentle kiss that conveyed his deep feelings. "Would it help you to know that I spoke to your uncle's solicitor and your dowry will be released within the month?"

Elinor beamed. "That is wonderful news. Have you considered where you want to buy up land?"

"I was thinking Kendal."

Elinor gave him a baffled look. "By my uncle?" she asked, her brow furrowing. "Why would you ever want to live by him?"

"He approached me about selling his country home, being as it is not entailed," Alden said, his eyes steady on Elinor's. "I thought you might want it."

Her eyes went wide. "Are you in earnest?"

"I am," Alden replied.

In the next moment, Elinor pulled him into a tight embrace. "Thank you, Alden. I can't even begin to explain what this means to me."

Alden smiled. "I take it that it pleases you."

"It does," Elinor declared.

Just then, the door to the stables opened, and a footman stood in the entryway, looking slightly hesitant. "I apologize for the interruption, but Lady Edith has come to call."

Alden's brow shot up. "My great-aunt is here?"

"Yes, sir," the footman confirmed. "She is waiting in the drawing room."

Elinor dropped her arms but quickly reached for his hand. "We mustn't keep her waiting," she said as she practically dragged him out of the stables.

Once they arrived at the manor, Alden followed Elinor

into the drawing room and saw his white-haired great-aunt gracefully sitting on one of the camelback settees. Her body looked frail and tired, but her eyes sparkled with liveliness.

When she saw them, she rose slowly and held her arms up. "My dear Elinor," she greeted warmly.

Elinor hurried over to her and threw her arms around Lady Edith. "It is so good to see you, my lady," she said, her voice brimming with affection.

"My lady? Since when have you started standing on formalities," Lady Edith said before turning towards Alden. "And how are you?"

"I am well," he replied.

Great-aunt Edith waved him forward with a playful gesture. "Do I not at least get a kiss on the cheek since I gave you a horse farm?"

"Yes, of course," Alden said, moving to kiss his great-aunt's cheek.

Once he had done so, he waited until the ladies sat before he claimed the seat next to Elinor.

Great-aunt Edith beamed at both of them. "It makes my heart happy to see you two together," she said. "I knew the moment I met Elinor that she would be perfect for you, Alden."

"You did?" Alden asked, slightly incredulous.

Great-aunt Edith nodded. "Yes, and I had to come up with the perfect reason to bring you two together," she said. "Furthermore, you have always been rather cocky, especially when it came to the ladies, and I knew that Elinor would knock you down a peg or two. Was I right?"

Elinor giggled. "You were," she agreed.

Alden shrugged, trying to hide his own amusement. "I am a smart enough man not to argue with that."

Mrs. Hardy entered the room and sat down next to Aunt Edith. "I am happy to see that you do not look worse for the wear," she said, her words light.

Lady Edith merely smiled. "I meant to arrive earlier, but I had to stop in York to speak to my great-niece, Rose."

"How is she faring?" Alden asked.

"With any luck, she is married now," Lady Edith said. "We had a good heart to heart talk, and I hope she heeds my advice. Unlike Cecilia did."

Mrs. Hardy looked the epitome of innocence. "In what way did I not heed your advice?"

"When I told you that I intended to play matchmaker with Elinor and Alden, I said to make yourself scarce, not dress up like a ghost," Lady Edith remarked.

Not appearing perturbed by Lady Edith's chiding, Mrs. Hardy responded, "It worked, did it not? It gave them the opportunity to speak freely."

The lines around Lady Edith's eyes crinkled with amusement. "I suppose it did," she admitted, turning back towards Alden. "My solicitor will arrive shortly with the deed to the horse farm and papers to transfer it to you. I do hope you will take good care of it."

Alden tipped his head. "*We* have every intention of doing so."

Great-aunt Edith's face softened with satisfaction. "I am so glad that you two found one another. Love is not something one should take for granted."

Reaching for Elinor's hand, Alden said, "I always thought I was destined for a loveless marriage like my parents, but then I met Elinor. I found that she is the one person that I can't live without."

"Then my work here is done," Great-aunt Edith declared, rising. "I need to take a nap from my long journey, but we shall continue this conversation later."

"Come, I shall show you to the guest bedchamber," Mrs. Hardy said, offering her arm to Lady Edith.

Once they had departed from the room, Elinor shifted to

face him, her eyes shining with affection. "You manage to say the nicest things to me."

"It is merely the truth," Alden said, leaning closer to her. "Life led me on a journey to you- one that I would never have gone on if it wasn't for Great-aunt Edith. I owe her everything."

Elinor pressed her lips against his in a tender kiss before pulling back slightly to whisper, "I love you."

"I love you, too, my love," Alden murmured, wrapping his arms around her. He didn't know what his future held, but he knew that Elinor held his future.

The End

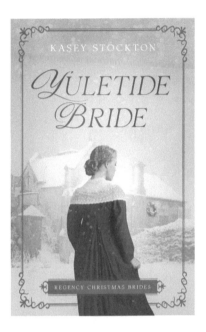

When a marriage of convenience becomes inconveniently complicated...

Mercy Caldwell, the vicar's eldest daughter, has watched her younger sisters march down the aisle while she remains resolutely on the shelf. When a chance at matrimony arrives mere hours after her youngest sister's engagement, Mercy seizes the opportunity—and the man she's secretly admired for years.

Colin Birchall's grand estate is crumbling, and his aunt's generous inheritance comes with one condition: he must be married by Twelfth Night. In Mercy, he finds the perfect candidate to meet his aunt's exacting standards. It seems an ideal arrangement—until they're forced to actually live together.

From differing views on marriage to clashing Christmas traditions, Mercy and Colin discover that convenience and compatibility are two very different things. But when Colin's aunt arrives unannounced demanding proof of their love, they must convince her—and perhaps themselves—that their hastily forged union is more than just a festive facade.

Also by Laura Beers

The Beckett Files

Regency Brides: A Promise of Love

Proper Regency Matchmakers

Regency Spies & Secrets

Gentlemen of London

Lords & Ladies of Mayfair

The Lockwood Family

About the Author

Laura Beers is an award-winning author. She attended Brigham Young University, earning a Bachelor of Science degree in Construction Management. She can't sing, doesn't dance and loves naps.

Laura lives in Utah with her husband, three kids, and her dysfunctional dog. When not writing regency romance, she loves skiing, hiking, and drinking Dr Pepper.

You can connect with Laura on Facebook, Instagram, or on her site at www.authorlaurabeers.com.

Made in United States
Troutdale, OR
11/11/2024